Kissing Paige ~~was not the~~
smartest thing he'd ever done.

On the other hand, he knew it had been inevitable, that they had been moving inexorably toward this moment since he'd walked her home from the town hall debate earlier in the week.

One kiss—just to prove to himself that she didn't have the same hold on him that she used to. Except that one kiss had proven him wrong. She tasted just like he remembered—right down to the cherry lip balm she'd favored when she was sixteen. Just one kiss, and he knew that he wanted her as much now as he'd always wanted her.

Maybe even more....

* * *

**Montana Mavericks: Rust Creek Cowboys:
Better saddle up. It's going to be a bumpy ride!**

Dear Reader,

I love reunion stories and I've loved the Montana Mavericks series since the beginning, so I was thrilled by the invitation to be part of this latest expansion of the continuity—Rust Creek Cowboys.

I grew up in a small town, where a five-minute trip to the corner store inevitably led to crossing paths with a friend or family member or acquaintance and resulted in a thirty-minute conversation. Rust Creek Falls is that kind of town, where everyone knows everyone else—and everyone knows at least something of the history between Sutter Traub and Paige Dalton.

But it *is* history—or so Paige has tried to convince herself. After all, Sutter left town five years earlier and she's moved on with her life without him. But when he comes back to Rust Creek Falls, there is no denying the sparks that fly between the stable owner and the schoolteacher. Add in some holiday season ambience and Paige starts to wonder what might happen if she manages to get this *Maverick under the Mistletoe!*

I hope you enjoy their story.

Happy Reading!

Brenda Harlen

A Maverick under the Mistletoe

Brenda Harlen

H HARLEQUIN® SPECIAL EDITION®

Special thanks and acknowledgment to Brenda Harlen for her contribution to the Montana Mavericks: Rust Creek Cowboys continuity.

Recycling programs
for this product may
not exist in your area.

ISBN-13: 978-0-373-65775-9

A MAVERICK UNDER THE MISTLETOE

Printed in U.S.A.

BRENDA HARLEN

is a former family law attorney turned work-at-home mom and national bestselling author who has written more than twenty books for Harlequin. Her work has been validated by industry awards (including an RWA Golden Heart® Award and the *RT Book Reviews* Reviewers' Choice Award) and by the fact that her kids think it's cool that she's "a real author."

Brenda lives in southern Ontario with her husband and two sons. When she isn't at the computer working on her next book, she can probably be found at the arena, watching a hockey game. Keep up-to-date with Brenda on Facebook or send her an email at brendaharlen@yahoo.com.

To Chris R., Christyne, Leanne, Karen and Vikki—
brainstormers, researchers and community planners
extraordinaire. Thanks for making the writing of
this book not just easier but a lot more fun.

To Susan Litman—for keeping us on track
while still letting us color outside of the lines.
(And yes, I know that's a mixed metaphor ☺)

With thanks also to my good friend Anna Perrin,
who always has the solutions to my last-minute plot
problems (even if I can't always use them).

Chapter One

In Sutter Traub's opinion, Rust Creek Falls was as irresistible—and fickle—as a woman. Once upon a time his heart had belonged to this town and he couldn't have imagined ever living anywhere else. Then she'd turned him out and turned her back on him.

Just like the only woman he'd ever loved.

Of course, he'd come back when she'd needed him— the town, that was, not the woman. Because Paige Dalton had *never* needed him, and she wouldn't ever ask for his help if she did, and thinking about her now was only going to stir up memories and feelings he didn't want stirred up.

So he focused his attention on the reason that he was standing in the back corner of town hall now: the imminent election. When his brother Collin had recently announced his intention to run for mayor of Rust Creek Falls, Sutter had impulsively volunteered to be his campaign manager. Which had resulted in him spending a lot more time in town over the past few months than he'd ever intended when news of the floods had first brought him home, which meant that he wasn't going back to Seattle before the last ballot was counted.

But for now he just wanted this debate to be over.

It was the last public face-off between the two mayoral candidates—Collin Traub and Nathan Crawford— before the citizens of Rust Creek Falls went to the polls on Thursday, and though it had just gotten underway, Sutter wished it was already done.

He couldn't have said why, but he had an uneasy feeling about the event. It might have had something to do with Nate's smug expression when they'd been setting up. It was as if he had something up his sleeve and, knowing the Crawfords, Sutter didn't doubt it for a minute.

As the debate progressed, he gradually began to relax. Collin was comfortable in front of the crowd, answering questions easily and confidently. He had a clearly defined plan to return Rust Creek Falls to its former glory and he made sure the residents knew it. Nate focused more on the history of the town than its future, and more on why he was the better candidate to fix the problems than how he was going to do so. But both candidates were—at least to all outward appearances—respectful of one another, and the spectators seemed to be listening to each side.

But when Thelma McGee—the former mayor's mother and moderator of the event—stood up to announce that the debate was finished, a member of the audience loudly pushed back his chair and rose to his feet.

A Crawford supporter, Sutter immediately suspected, and the gleam in Nate's eyes made him think that there was nothing spontaneous about the man's actions.

He was a military man in a dress uniform with his medals proudly displayed on his chest, and Sutter's heart immediately began to pound. One sleeve of the man's uniform hung loose because he had no arm to put through it. Not just a decorated veteran but a wounded war hero.

Perspiration beaded on Sutter's brow and trickled down his spine.

Thelma, bless her, never wavered. "I'm sorry, sir—"

"Master Sergeant Dean Riddell." He barked out the name as if it was a military order.

"Yes, well, we've run out of time tonight and—"

"Time is irrelevant when our boys are fighting to protect our freedoms. And I want to remind the good people of Rust Creek Falls that they need to know if these candidates support our armed forces."

"While your concern is acknowledged and appreciated, the eventual mayor of Rust Creek Falls has no voice with respect to military activity or spending. This is strictly about local politics."

While Sutter heard and silently applauded her point, no one else did, because they'd all started talking and debating among themselves.

"Ladies and gentlemen—" Collin tried to settle the crowd while Nate just sat back with his arms folded across his chest and a smug smile on his face. "Do I need to remind you that my brother, Major Forrest Traub, is a decorated war hero, too? He fought valiantly and tirelessly for his country—for all of us—and I have never been anything but supportive of his efforts and his sacrifices."

"Can you say the same thing about your campaign manager?" the master sergeant demanded.

And Sutter knew the damage had been done. It didn't matter that everything Collin said was true; what mattered to these people was that there was mud to be slung—and it was Sutter's fault that Collin was the one wearing it.

He'd been young and impetuous and probably a little too outspoken in his efforts to convince his brother that he'd already gone above and beyond in the service of his country. He'd vehemently objected when Forrest had announced his intention to reenlist for another tour, because he'd just wanted his brother to stay home and be safe.

But Forrest had chosen to go back, and when he returned to Rust Creek Falls again after his medical discharge, Sutter had known the scars on his brother's leg were insignificant compared to the damage to his soul. Thankfully, months of physical therapy and falling in love with Angie Anderson had started healing his body and his heart—but his relationship with his brother was going to need something more.

Obviously no one in Rust Creek Falls had forgotten Sutter's objections. And while he acknowledged and accepted that he would always be haunted by the mistakes of his past, he hadn't expected that anyone else would have to pay for his outspokenness. Listening to the crowd, now thoroughly stirred up by Master Sergeant Riddell, he finally realized that his presence could hinder Collin's campaign rather than help—exactly as Nate Crawford had intended.

They were still murmuring and bickering when another spectator stood up on the other side of the room. And Sutter's heart began to pound even harder inside his chest when he recognized Paige Dalton.

He hadn't seen her enter the hall, hadn't known she was there. That in and of itself was a surprise, because Sutter had always had a sixth sense where Paige was concerned. A sixth sense that had been honed by self-preservation since his return to Rust Creek Falls a few months earlier.

Looking at her now, she took his breath away. It wasn't just that she was beautiful, but the way she stood—with her spine stiff and her chin up—she looked like a warrior ready to take on the entire population of Rust Creek Falls, or at least those who were assembled in town hall tonight. She was wearing a soft pink peasant-style blouse over a raspberry-colored skirt. Her long, dark brown hair hung straight down to the middle of her back, and her dark chocolate-colored eyes were focused and intense.

He braced himself for her attack. He didn't care what Master Sergeant Riddell or anyone else in Rust Creek Falls thought about him—except insofar as it might impact Collin's hopes of winning the election—but he'd never stopped caring about Paige and he hated knowing that she was disappointed in him.

"Can we focus on what's relevant here?" she said to the crowd. She didn't yell—in fact, she raised her voice just enough to be heard. And as she continued to speak, her volume dropped further, forcing others to stop talking in order to hear what she was saying. "First, and most important, is the fact that it is *Collin* Traub who is running for office, not Sutter.

"Second, regardless of whether any of us agree with statements that Sutter made with respect to his brother's decision to reenlist five years ago, those statements were *his opinion,* it was *five years ago,* and we need to *focus on the issues* that are relevant to Rust Creek Falls *in the present* and the *candidates who are actually running* in this election."

She paused a moment to take a breath and to give everyone a minute to think about what she'd said before she continued. "But even if it was Sutter instead of Collin who was running for mayor, he would get my vote because he's the type of man who's willing to stand up for what he believes, regardless of popular opinion or what anyone else might think. That is a man of conviction, and that is the kind of man who gets things done, and what Rust Creek Falls needs right now is someone who can get things done.

"Thankfully, that is a trait he shares with his brother Collin. And that is why *Collin* Traub is the type of man we need in charge of our town during this difficult time.

"With all due respect, Master Sergeant Riddell, the

army isn't coming here to rebuild our town. And I think you would agree that our servicemen and women have more important things to do. That leaves it up to *us,* the citizens of Rust Creek Falls, to figure out the best way to get things done—and the best person to help us do so. I think that person is Collin Traub."

Then she picked up her jacket and calmly turned to walk down the aisle between the folding chairs and out the door.

"Thank you again for your time tonight—"

Thelma McGee was speaking again, but Sutter didn't hang around to listen to what the moderator said. He needed to see Paige. He wasn't entirely sure why, he just knew that he did.

He slipped out through a side door and raced around to the front of the building. Paige couldn't have had more than a two-minute head start on him, but she seemed to have vanished into thin air. He scanned the dimly lit street and finally spotted her when she neared a lamp-post at the end of the block.

"Paige—wait!"

She paused at the corner of North Main Street and as he drew nearer, he saw the reluctance on her face. She looked as if she'd rather bolt than wait, but she held her ground until he reached her side. Then she turned east up Cedar Street, obviously wanting to be out of sight of town hall when the crowd dispersed.

He didn't blame her for not wanting to be seen with him. They'd both grown up in this town where almost everyone knew everyone else, and it was safe to assume that most of the residents knew at least some of Sutter and Paige's history together.

"I just wanted to thank you," he said when he fell into step beside her.

"I didn't do it for you," she told him.

"Why did you do it?"

"Because Nate's been running an underhanded campaign since Collin threw his hat into the ring, but dragging a war veteran into this debate solely to discredit your brother..." She trailed off, shaking her head. "That's a new low, even for Nate."

"Are you sure he set it up?"

"I saw him talking to the master sergeant before the debate," she confided. "I have absolutely no doubt that he planted him in the audience to stir up trouble."

"Well, I don't think the tactic was nearly as successful as he'd hoped, not after your little speech."

She shrugged. "I was there because I want to be an informed voter. My personal bias aside, I wanted to hear what the candidates had to say, how they responded to questions. Everything I saw and heard tonight confirmed my belief that Collin is the best mayoral candidate, and I wanted to make sure that people left the hall talking about him—not you."

"Well, I appreciate what you said, anyway," he told her. "I know it couldn't have been easy to speak up in my defense—even if it was for my brother—after... everything."

After...everything.

Sutter's words echoed in Paige's mind, making her wonder if that was really how he thought about the fact that he'd broken her heart and shattered her hopes and dreams. Had their relationship been so meaningless, and their breakup so inconsequential to him, that he could just categorize those events as "everything"?

She looked up at him, amazed and annoyed that even after five years a simple glance was enough to make her heart pound. Of course, he probably had that effect on a lot of women. At six feet two inches, with the solid, muscular build of a real cowboy, he turned heads no matter where he went. The thick, light brown hair, deep blue eyes and quick smile kept those heads turned in his direction. She deliberately tore her gaze away.

It infuriated her that after five years, her heart was still aching from his callous dismissal, while he seemed completely unaffected. But there was no way she was going to ask for clarification. Instead she only said, "It was a long time ago."

"Was it?" he challenged, his voice quieter now and tinged with a hint of sadness.

Or maybe she was only hearing what she wanted to hear.

"I'll admit, there are days when it seems like our relationship was in a different lifetime," he told her. "And there are other days when I would swear it was only yesterday. When I can close my eyes and see you right in front of me, reach out as if to touch the softness of your skin, breathe in and catch the scent of your perfume."

She wouldn't let the soft seduction of his words or his voice sway her. "I think you've been breathing in something that's not legal in this state without a prescription."

"Ouch—that was harsh."

"What kind of response did you expect?"

"I don't know," he admitted. "Maybe I just wanted to know that you think about me sometimes, too."

"I don't. Because it wasn't yesterday—it was five years ago, and I have too much going on in my life right now to think about what used to be or might have been."

But her words were a lie. The truth was, she didn't just think about Sutter sometimes. She thought about him far too often. It didn't seem to matter that he'd been gone for five years, because her heart had never quite healed. And even after all that time, whenever she saw him—which, thankfully, hadn't been very often before the horrible flood had brought him back to Rust Creek Falls—it felt like ripping the scab off of the wound.

And yet when a stranger who didn't even know him started attacking his character, Paige couldn't seem to help herself from flying to his defense. Because regardless of what had happened between them, she knew that deep inside Sutter was a good man. The man she'd once loved more than anything.

"So tell me what's going on in your life," he said now.

She turned to look at him. "Why?"

"Because I want to know."

"Well, I've been teaching my fifth-grade class in my living room because we don't have a school anymore—which is one of the reasons I'm so invested in the outcome of this election. We need to get the new school built because our kids deserve better than what we've been able to do for them so far."

"Fifth grade?" Sutter frowned. "I think Dallas's eldest is in fifth grade."

She nodded. "Ryder's in my class."

"He's had a rough go of it…since his mother walked out."

"It hasn't been easy on any of the boys." She felt herself softening in response to his obvious concern about his nephew, just a little, and steeled herself against it. "But when one person walks out of a relationship, it's inevitable that someone else is going to be hurt."

His gaze narrowed. "Are we still talking about Ryder?"

"Of course," she agreed, the picture of innocence. "Who else would we be talking about?"

"Us," he said bluntly. "I thought you might have

been referring to the end of our relationship—when you dumped me."

She hated that he could still see through her so easily. "I wasn't talking about us, and I didn't dump you," she denied. "I simply refused to run away with you. Because that's what you did—you ran."

"I'm back now," he told her.

And standing close to him, it was all too easy for Paige to remember the way she used to feel about him. Far too easy to want to feel that way again. Thankfully she wasn't a naive teenager anymore, and she wouldn't let it happen. Because sooner or later Sutter would leave Rust Creek Falls again. He always did.

"Yes, you're back now," she acknowledged. "But for how long?"

Sutter's gaze slid away. "Well, as Collin's campaign manager, I'll be hanging around until the election."

His response was hardly unexpected, and yet Paige couldn't deny that she felt a pang of disappointment in response to his words. "Yeah, that's what I thought."

"It's not easy being here," he reminded her. "No one has ever welcomed me back with open arms."

She would have. If he'd come home at any time during those first six months that he'd been gone, she would have welcomed him with open arms and a heart so full of love for him that it was near to bursting.

But he hadn't come home, not at all in the first year or for a very long time after. And the longer he was gone, the more she realized that the overwhelming love she felt for him wasn't reciprocated—at least not in the way she needed it to be if they were going to build a life together.

Instead, they'd each moved on without the other. By all accounts Sutter was doing very well in Seattle. Apparently he'd opened his own stables in the city and had established quite the reputation for himself. Paige had been sincerely happy to hear the news and genuinely pleased for him, because she was more than content with her own life in Rust Creek Falls.

She loved her job, she lived close enough to her family that she saw them regularly—although she sometimes wondered if maybe a little *too* frequently—she had good friends and she even went out on occasion. She didn't want or need anything more—and she certainly didn't want Sutter Traub turning her life upside down again.

"You saw that tonight," he pointed out to her. "No one has forgotten what happened, why I left, and no one will miss me when I'm gone again."

She could tell that he believed it, and her heart ached for him. "This is your home," she told him. "Whether you choose to live here or not, this is where you belong—with your family and your friends and everyone else who cares about you."

He managed a wry smile, but his tone when he responded was more wistful than skeptical. "Would you be included in that list?"

Chapter Two

"Of course," Paige agreed. "Despite everything that's happened between us, we've always been friends."

Even as the words tumbled out of her mouth, she wished she could haul them back. Because as much as she believed coming home and making peace with his family was the right thing for Sutter, she knew it wouldn't work out so well for her. Not when even this brief conversation had her churned up inside.

"Well, speaking in confidence to a friend," Sutter said, "I'm afraid Collin's fighting an uphill battle in this election."

She was surprised, and grateful, for the change of topic. "What makes you say that?"

"The fact that every time I go into town, I hear rumblings—and none of them are very subtle."

"What kind of rumblings?"

"Just the other day I was at the general store and I heard Ginny Nigh comment to Lilah Goodwin that it's a sorry state when people nowadays don't understand the importance of family values. It used to be that when a man got a woman pregnant, he did the right thing and married the mother of his child."

"You think she was talking about Clayton?"

"I know she was. Of course, she didn't mention the fact that Clay didn't even know Delia was pregnant until she showed up on his doorstep with the baby—or the fact that Delia turned around and hightailed it out of town only a few days later."

"Leaving your brother with the son he never knew he had—which, to me, proves that he *does* understand family values. He stepped right up to be a daddy to Bennett and never tried to pawn him off on anybody else."

He smiled, just a little. "I wish you'd been at the store with me."

But of course they both knew that such an occurrence would have generated gossip of a different kind.

"Anyway, you shouldn't worry about Ginny—everyone knows she's just an old busybody."

"Unfortunately, she isn't the only one who's been talking. Even the minister in church the other day was talking about wedding vows and that 'till death do us part' needs to mean till death and not until one of the spouses decides he or she has had enough."

"Pastor Alderson has never made any secret of the fact that he's opposed to divorce."

"And Dallas is divorced—but he only took the step to end his marriage after his wife walked out on him and the kids."

"I think most people around here know that the divorce was instigated by Laurel's abandonment."

"Do they?" he challenged. "Or do they see it as proof that the Traubs don't reflect the traditional family values that are a cornerstone of Rust Creek Falls?"

"Collin has to pick his battles," Paige said reasonably. "He can't expect to win every argument on every issue, so he should focus on what he's doing and not worry about rumors."

"That's what we've been trying to do," Sutter admitted. "The purpose of his national online initiative to help rebuild Rust Creek Falls was designed to give people a reason to look past the devastation and focus on the positive."

"'A vote for Collin Traub is a vote for success and prosperity for the future of Rust Creek Falls,'" she quoted.

He grinned. "You've been reading our press."

"I've been reading everything in the press," she clarified. "I like to make an informed decision."

"Are you seeing anyone?"

She stopped in the middle of the sidewalk, stunned by the abrupt change of topic. "How is that any of your business?"

"Maybe it's not," he admitted. "But I heard that you've been keeping company with a foreman at the lumber mill, and I want to know if it's true."

"It's true." She started walking again. "I've been dating Alex Monroe for a few months now."

"Is it serious?"

"Again—none of your business," she said, because she wasn't going to admit to Sutter that her relationship with the other man wasn't anywhere close to being serious.

Alex was a great guy. He was attractive and well mannered and she enjoyed spending time with him. Unfortunately there was no real spark or sizzle between them, nothing to make her think that their relationship would ever progress to the next level.

Her sisters, Lani and Lindsay, claimed that Paige wouldn't ever be able to have a serious relationship with Alex—or any other man—so long as she was still carrying a torch for Sutter. She, of course, denied that was true, because she'd given up hope that Sutter would come back to her a long time ago.

But standing beside him now, she was suddenly overwhelmed by the memories of what they'd once shared, and she realized that maybe she had been comparing other men to "the one who got away." But she didn't think that was so unusual. After all, Sutter had been her first love and her first lover, and she couldn't imagine any subsequent relationship having that same depth and intensity.

And she wasn't going to waste even another minute of her time worrying about it tonight. She started walking again, and he fell into step beside her.

A few minutes later, she paused outside a two-story saltbox-style house with steel-blue clapboard siding and wide white trim around the front door and windows.

"This is mine," she said, and felt a familiar thrill when she spoke those words. Two years earlier, when she'd put in her offer for the house, she'd been excited—and then absolutely terrified when it was accepted. Gradually the terror had subsided, beaten back by endless weeks and months of intense manual labor to scrub and shine and prep and paint until she felt as if it was well and truly her own.

He gave the house a quick once-over. "Nice," he said approvingly.

She didn't want or need his approval, but she found herself smiling anyway. Because it *was* nice. More important, it was hers.

"Are you going to invite me in for coffee?" he asked.

"No."

His brows lifted. "Just no? You're not even going to make up some kind of lame excuse as to why you can't invite me in?"

"I don't need to make up an excuse," she told him. "The fact is, tomorrow is a school day and I have lesson plans to review."

The smile that flashed across his face actually made her knees weak.

"For a minute it was almost like we were back in high school," he said.

She'd thought the same thing as soon as the words were out of her mouth. There had been a lot of times when Sutter had tried to convince her to stay out with him instead of going home to finish her homework or study for an upcoming test. And a lot of times when she'd let herself be convinced. And when he'd finally walked her home, they'd still been reluctant to part, so they'd stood in the shadows of the back porch of her parents' house and kissed good-night. He'd spent a lot of time kissing her good-night.

Obviously he was remembering the same thing, because he took a step closer and said, "Are you going to let me kiss you good-night?"

"No." Though she knew she should hold her ground, she took an instinctive step back.

Sutter smiled knowingly. "Are you busy Thursday night?"

This second abrupt change in topic made her almost as wary as his previous request. "Why?"

"It's election night," he reminded her. "And the candidates and their supporters will be gathered at town hall for the results. Since you've declared your support for Collin, I thought you might want to be there."

She did believe Collin was the best candidate and he was definitely going to get her vote, but hanging out with his family and friends at town hall meant being around Sutter, and she wasn't sure if that was something she could handle.

"I'll think about it," she finally agreed, because once he'd made the offer, she knew that she wouldn't be able to not think about it. But she also knew that there was no way she could go.

The only hope she had of protecting her heart was to stay as far away from Sutter Traub as possible.

Since it wasn't an outright refusal, Sutter decided not to press Paige for a firm commitment. He simply waited until she'd unlocked her door, then he wished her a good night and headed back to town hall. He hadn't realized how far they'd walked until he had to make the trek back again without the pleasure of her company.

He'd enjoyed walking and talking with her like they'd done so many times before. But that was the past. He retraced his steps as he'd lived the past five years of his life—without her. And he tried not to think about everything they'd once meant to one another, and everything they'd lost.

Paige Dalton had been his soul mate and best friend. His heart had belonged to her, wholly and completely. She was the one woman he'd imagined spending the rest of his life with. He'd even proposed marriage before he'd left town, but she'd turned him down and turned her back on him, and he'd gone to Washington alone.

The transition from Rust Creek Falls to Seattle hadn't been an easy one, and for the first several months Sutter had doubted it would be a successful one. He'd tried working at various office jobs in the city, but he never found one that seemed to fit. Or maybe he was just too restless to sit behind a desk all day. It was only when he heard about a job opening for a horse trainer at a local stable that things began to turn around for him.

He'd always been good with animals and he'd quickly established a reputation for himself with the local horse set. After a couple of years working for someone else, he had both the money and the confidence he needed to venture out on his own.

Three years earlier, he'd opened Traub Stables, and he was gratified by its success. He was also pleased that his business had created a second market for CT Saddles—Collin's custom-made saddles and leather-goods business. That was all Sutter wanted—all he needed. Or so he'd believed until he'd come back to Rust Creek Falls again.

When he'd left town five years earlier, he'd vowed that he would never return. Of course, he'd been younger and more impulsive then, and the simple fact that his family was in Rust Creek Falls guaranteed that he wouldn't be able to stay away forever. Despite the harsh words that had been thrown around in the Traub household, he could never really turn his back on his family—even if he felt they'd turned their backs on him first.

So when he'd heard the news about the flood, he had to come home to make sure everything was okay at the ranch. Of course, it had taken him some time to get everything in order with his business so that he could feel comfortable leaving for a couple of weeks. And even then, his apprehension had increased with every mile that drew him closer to the Triple T. There was still tension in his family—most notably between Sutter and Forrest—and it had occurred to him that he might not be welcome. Especially if his war-hero brother had also decided to return.

Both Forrest and Clayton were living in Thunder Canyon these days with their new wives and, in Clayton's case, children. But Sutter was certain they would also be drawn back to Rust Creek Falls, eager to do anything they could to help out not just the Traub family but the larger community.

Another reason that Sutter had questioned his impulse to return was the possibility that he might run into

Paige Dalton. A possibility that had turned into a certainty when he found out that Collin was marrying Willa Christensen—a friend and colleague of Paige's.

Of his five brothers, Collin was the only one who got Sutter and who hadn't judged him for his less-than-enthusiastic support of Forrest's decision to return to Iraq. So when Collin had asked Sutter to be his best man, he hadn't even considered refusing. He hadn't found out until later that Paige would be Willa's maid of honor.

The wedding had been simple but beautiful. And Sutter and Paige had both focused on their respective duties and pretended to be oblivious to one another. At least, Sutter was pretending. And he'd *tried* to focus on his duties, but Paige had always been a distraction.

She was the most beautiful girl he'd ever known. Now that girl was a woman and even more of a distraction. Willa had been a gorgeous bride, and Sutter had been thrilled to see his brother so obviously in love and more contented than he'd ever been, but it was the bride's maid of honor who had caught—and held—Sutter's attention.

Her long dark hair had been fashioned into some kind of loose knot on top of her head, but a few strands had escaped to frame her delicate heart-shaped face. Her dark eyes had been enhanced with makeup, her sharp cheekbones highlighted and her sweetly curved lips had been painted a glossy pink color.

Her dress was a long, strapless column of pale lilac silk that hugged her curves. She'd been more skinny than thin as a girl, but there was no doubt she was a woman now. A woman with silky-smooth skin and beautiful shoulders that had seemed rather chilly whenever she'd turned them in his direction.

Unfortunately, her obvious disinterest had done nothing to cool the blood running through his veins. But he'd managed to get through the wedding without giving in to the desire to touch her, and he'd breathed a sigh of relief when the event was over.

He'd done a pretty good job of avoiding Paige in the months that had passed since then—until tonight, when his need just to see her and talk to her had overridden his common sense and sent him chasing after her.

When he'd offered to manage Collin's campaign, he'd claimed it was simply because he believed that his brother truly was the best person for the job—especially considering that the only other candidate was Nathan Crawford. He hadn't been willing to admit, even to himself, that Paige Dalton had been a factor in his decision to stay in Rust Creek Falls a little longer. Maybe he'd been an idiot where she was concerned, but he wasn't a masochist. Once bitten, twice shy and all that.

But now, three months later, he was still in Rust Creek Falls and still hoping to catch a glimpse of her around every corner. And that, he knew, was a definite sign that it was long past time to go back to Seattle.

He'd been making occasional trips back and forth, not so much to keep an eye on his business, because he trusted his stable manager absolutely, but to ensure that he was able to give the personal touch to his major clients. But he'd never stayed in Seattle more than a few days before he'd found a reason to return to Rust Creek Falls again. He decided now that he needed to get back to his real life before he let himself start believing that he could ever come home to stay. Because the more time he spent here, the more he remembered how it had felt to be part of the close-knit community, and the more he craved that sense of belonging again.

The town had come together and had made impressive headway with respect to the repairs that were needed.

It never ceased to amaze him how people managed to overcome their differences and work together in times of crisis. In fact, Collin and Nate had worked side by side on the Recovery Committee with Sheriff Gage Christensen—Willa's brother—and Thelma McGee.

Sutter had pitched in wherever help was needed and, as a result, had occasionally crossed paths with Paige. Each time he saw her, he was reminded of what they'd once had—and what he'd lost. And almost every night since his return, he dreamed of her when he went to sleep.

That was just one more reason that he was looking forward to going back to Seattle—so he could sleep through the night without dreams of a sexy, dark-eyed brunette disturbing his slumber. Not that the distance had helped him forget about Paige completely, but it had forced him to accept that she'd chosen a life without him. And he knew the best thing for him now was to get back to that life without her. Except that he'd made his brother a promise, and that meant that Sutter was going to be in Rust Creek Falls until the last ballot was counted.

His faith in his brother had not wavered once since Collin had announced his candidacy. If anything, the more he learned about his brother's plans and ideas for the town, the more convinced he was that Collin was the right man to lead Rust Creek Falls through this crisis and toward a better, stronger future. Unfortunately, instead of promoting his own ideas, Nathan Crawford was more interested in slinging mud at the Traubs.

For some reason that Sutter couldn't even pretend to understand, the Traubs and the Crawfords had been at odds for generations. According to the widely circulated rumors around town, the feud had originated with a business partnership gone wrong. Of course, that was only one version of the story and, depending on the telling, even it had several variations and discrepancies as to which party had done the wrong.

In any event, the animosity that existed between the families since before Sutter could remember had come to a head a few years earlier when Collin and Nate had gotten into a fight over accusations that Nate's girlfriend was stepping out with his nemesis. Collin's announcement that he would run against Nate in the election had further exacerbated the tensions.

"Where did you disappear to?" Collin demanded when Sutter finally got back to town hall.

The majority of the crowd had dispersed, leaving only a handful of people in the building: volunteers stacking up chairs and sweeping the floors, Willa in conversation with a young couple who were just as likely to be talking to her about their daughter who was in her kindergarten class as an issue regarding Collin's campaign.

"I needed some air," Sutter told his brother.

"You didn't follow Paige?"

He scowled. "I'm not a stalker, but yes, I did talk to her. I wanted to thank her for the things she said."

"Her words did interject rationale and reason into an uncomfortable situation—at least for the moment."

"She promised that you have her vote," Sutter told him.

"I'm grateful for that," Collin said. "But I'm more concerned about you."

"You've got my vote, too."

His brother cuffed the side of Sutter's head. "I meant that I'm concerned about you and Paige."

"There is no me and Paige—there hasn't been for a long time." Of course, knowing that fact didn't stop him from thinking about her—or wanting her. "Besides, she's seeing Alex Monroe."

"I know that she's gone out with him a few times," Collin admitted. "I don't know that it's exclusive, though."

"It doesn't matter," Sutter insisted. "My life is in Seattle now, and she made it clear a long time ago that she has no intention of ever leaving Rust Creek Falls."

"Your business is in Seattle," his brother agreed. "But your family is here."

"Now you sound like Paige," he grumbled.

"Really?" Collin seemed intrigued by the idea. "Well, where you choose to live is your decision. I just want to be sure that you're not planning to go anywhere before the election."

"I'm not, unless you want me to."

"I don't."

"That whole scene tonight—it happened because of me."

"It happened because Nate Crawford doesn't know how to play by the rules."

Sutter couldn't deny that was true, but he still hated to think that his brother could lose the election because of him. Certainly the tide of popular opinion had turned against him in a heartbeat tonight, until Paige's timely interjection.

"Desperate times call for desperate measures," Willa said, coming over to join in their conversation. "And I think Nate is feeling more than a little desperate."

Collin slid his arm around her. "Why do you say that?"

"Because he knows he's going to lose this election, and the defeat is going to be that much harder to take for a Crawford beaten by a Traub."

"While I appreciate your confidence, you might want to hold off on the victory speech until the votes are actually counted," Collin told her.

Secretly, Sutter couldn't help but agree with his

brother. As much as he appreciated Willa's optimism about her new husband's chances in the election, he didn't share her faith. He truly believed Collin was the best candidate for the job, but Nate Crawford had run a clever campaign. Instead of focusing on his plans to return the town to its former glory—no doubt because he knew that Collin was leaps and bounds ahead of him in that regard—he'd chosen to focus on his family's place in the town's history, and on digging up dirt on his opponent.

Not that there was much dirt to be found on Collin, which was surely why Nate had expanded his smear campaign to encompass the whole of the Traub family. And in doing so, he'd had more success.

Sutter could only hope that Nate's efforts would be in vain.

Chapter Three

Sutter said goodbye to Collin and Willa and headed back to the Triple T. He bypassed the main house and went directly to Clayton's residence on the property. Since Clay had moved to Thunder Canyon, his place had become a guest house for visitors, and although Sutter wasn't technically a guest, he felt more comfortable there than in the main house.

Mostly he appreciated the privacy and the solitude, and he was grateful for both tonight. He didn't feel like making idle conversation with anyone, especially not his well-meaning but undeniably interfering mother, and especially not if she'd somehow gotten wind of the fact that Paige had been present at the town hall debate.

Ellie had always liked Paige, and despite the breakup with Sutter she hadn't yet given up hope that they might somehow find their way back to one another. So she made a point of keeping him apprised of what was going on in Paige's life—including the fact that she was dating the mill foreman.

Sutter knew that the information hadn't been intended to hurt him but to spur him into action, his mother expecting that he would charge into town and sweep Paige off her feet and into his arms again. Even if he'd thought such a grand gesture might be successful, Sutter knew that he had no right to interfere in her life now. Five years earlier, they'd made their own choices and gone their separate ways.

And now she was dating Alex Monroe.

That fact was more difficult to accept than he wanted to acknowledge. He didn't know Alex well, but he knew who he was and he had nothing against the guy. He just didn't like the idea of Paige with anyone else.

Which was admittedly hypocritical considering that he'd hardly lived like a monk in the five years since he'd left Rust Creek Falls. But the truth was, he hadn't been with anyone since Paige who had made him forget about her.

He'd fallen in love with her when he was barely seventeen, and with the innocence and conviction of youth, he'd been absolutely certain that he would love her forever. They'd talked about their future together, when they would get married, where they would live, how many children they wanted. And he'd believed that she loved him, too—right up until the moment she'd told him she couldn't marry him.

Even five years later, the memory of that impulsive and rejected proposal stung. Because even now he knew he wasn't completely over his feelings for Paige, while she seemed to have moved on without so much as a backward glance in his direction.

The fact that she'd bought a house proved to him that she still wanted most of the same things they'd talked about. That she hadn't let him get past the front door proved that he wasn't a factor in any of her plans.

Which, of course, made him wonder if Alex Monroe was. Had she invited him in for coffee? Had he been given a tour of Paige's house? Had he seen her bedroom? Spent the night in her bed?

Sutter scowled, acknowledging that those were questions he probably didn't want to know the answers to—even the speculation was making him crazy.

He deliberately turned his thoughts to why she'd moved out of her parents' house. Maybe she'd wanted to be closer to her job, although a couple of blocks hardly made a difference. In a town like Rust Creek Falls, commuting times were never a concern.

More likely she'd wanted her own space, more independence. Paige had always been close to her family, but she'd often chafed at their rules and restrictions. It was a common complaint of many teenagers, but she was a grown woman now, an incredibly beautiful woman living alone in a house that was probably just waiting for the children she'd always wanted.

He poured himself a glass of whiskey and swallowed it in a single gulp. The liquor burned a path down his throat and into his belly, but it didn't touch the aching emptiness in his heart. So he poured himself a second drink and was considering a third when he realized what he was doing. He pushed the bottle aside and headed to bed.

It had been a lot of years since he'd drunk himself into a stupor over a woman, and even that hadn't helped him forget either the pain or the loneliness. Of course, it had been Paige then, too, and he wasn't going to go down that path again.

It was a decision he found himself questioning later. If he'd consumed enough alcohol to pass out drunk, maybe he wouldn't have been able to dream. Because when he finally did fall asleep, his dreams were filled with images of Paige, past and present. Memories mingled with fantasy in an enticing montage that teased and tormented him through the night.

When he finally woke the next morning with his heart pounding and the sheets twisted around his body, he actually ached for her.

Teaching wasn't an easy job at the best of times, and these were definitely not the best of times. There was so much going on in the town, so many families who had been displaced and so many demands on Paige's time and attention that she sometimes didn't know which direction to turn. As if all of that wasn't enough, Sutter Traub had planted himself in the middle of everything by getting involved with his brother's mayoral campaign and churning up a lot of feelings she'd thought were long dead—or at least deeply buried.

She walked around the long table that had been set up in her living-room-turned-classroom to check on the mock campaign posters her students were creating. Early on in her teaching career, she'd realized that kids learned more easily and maintained information more readily when they could relate the lessons to real life, so she'd talked about the recent flood during a unit on environmental studies and had worked the upcoming election into their discussion about governments.

The latter had certainly given her some insights into the political leanings of many local families, and though the class seemed fairly evenly divided between "Team Crawford" and "Team Traub," she was optimistic that Collin would emerge victorious. But right now she tried to focus her thoughts not on the upcoming election but on the current lesson.

She really did love her job and looked forward to the start of every day, approaching each subject with equal enthusiasm. She had her own personal favorites, of course, but she tried not to let that bias show. She wanted her students to experience and enjoy everything. She loved being able to open their minds, to encourage their curiosity and nurture their creativity, and gloried in each and every one of their successes. And because she was so completely engaged with her students, she hurt when they were hurting.

And she knew that Ryder Traub was hurting. Sutter had been right about the fact that Dallas's eldest son was having a hard time adjusting to his mother's abandonment. He wasn't acting out, as was often the case with children going through difficult transitions. Instead, it was as if he'd drawn into himself, disengaging from the other students and the activities in the classroom. He wasn't uncooperative—he always did the work that was required of him—but Paige could tell that he was just going through the motions.

She tried to draw him out, but that wasn't an easy task when she had sixteen other students to attend to. Not that they all came to class every day, which was another reason teaching in her home was a challenge. It was as if the parents figured it wasn't an actual school, therefore, she couldn't actually be teaching. And that only made it harder to impress the importance of every lesson upon her students.

When the day was over and the last student had gone, she realized she needed more markers and stickers to replenish her cupboard. Sometimes she would go to the specialty classroom resource store in Kalispell, but for everyday supplies she could usually find what she needed at Crawford's General Store.

Unfortunately, she sometimes found more than she wanted, as was the situation when she realized it was Nate Crawford behind the counter instead of his sister.

She forced a smile as she emptied her basket. "Where's

Nina?" She wasn't just making conversation but was genuinely concerned about the woman, who was nearing the
end of her pregnancy.

"She had an appointment—" he automatically began
to scan Paige's purchases "—so I said I would cover the
store. It gives me a chance to connect with the people of
our town on a more personal basis."

Which Paige interpreted to mean that any poor soul
who wandered in for essential grocery items was likely
getting a healthy dose of Nate's campaign propaganda
along with every loaf of bread and quart of milk. "It
always helps the voters to know their candidates," she
agreed.

He totaled her order and she gave him her money.

He made change, but didn't immediately pass it across
the counter. "I feel as if I should warn you about something."

"I'm sure that's not necessary."

"I know you have…a history…with Sutter Traub," he
continued anyway. "But your public declaration of allegiance could make you unpopular in this town."

"I don't need to be popular—I'm not running for office." She picked up her bag and held out her hand for
her change.

"No," he agreed, finally giving her the money. "But
maybe your new boyfriend needs to know that you're
running around with your ex."

Paige knew that she'd done nothing wrong, that there
was absolutely no reason for her to feel as if she had, but
that knowledge didn't succeed in alleviating her guilt.
Because the truth was, the whole time she'd been with
Sutter the night before, she hadn't once thought about

Alex—not until Sutter had specifically asked her about the other man.

She didn't know if that said something about her relationship with the mill foreman or if it was simply a side effect of being near Sutter. She'd been dating Alex for a couple of months now and, after fifteen minutes in Sutter's company, she'd barely remembered his name. It was embarrassing to admit, even if only to herself, and Alex certainly deserved better than to be an afterthought.

So when she got home, she surveyed the contents of her refrigerator to ensure that she had the groceries she needed to put together a decent meal—because she was *not* going back to Crawford's for another dose of Nate's self-righteousness—then called Alex to invite him to come over for dinner. Though he seemed surprised by the impromptu invitation, he immediately accepted.

She set the table, even putting out candles and a bottle of wine, then set about preparing the meal. She was going to spend some time with Alex tonight and forget about Sutter Traub once and for all.

Sutter figured he must be a glutton for punishment. Why else would he have decided to drive down Cedar Street before he headed home the following night? It wasn't as if it was on his way. It wasn't really *out* of his way, but the most direct route would have been to continue along Main to Sawmill, since he had to cross the river at the Sawmill Street Bridge. Instead, he turned onto Cedar, then North Pine, so that he passed by Paige's house.

And in passing by Paige's house, he couldn't possibly miss the battered truck parked outside of it. He knew that the Cruze parked in front of it belonged to Paige, and he suspected that the truck belonged to Alex Monroe, because he'd seen the same vehicle in the parking lot at the mill every day. His mother had warned him that Paige was dating the foreman, and Paige herself had confirmed it, but he still hadn't wanted to believe it. But the truth was hard to deny when it was right in front of him.

She hadn't invited Sutter in for a cup of coffee the night before because it was a school night. Well, it was a school night tonight, too, and she didn't seem to have any qualms about having company. Or maybe she didn't consider Alex company. Maybe—

Don't go there.

He sharply reined in his wandering thoughts and continued on his way.

He'd honestly thought he'd let her go. When he'd driven away from Rust Creek Falls five years earlier and Paige had decided to stay, he'd known that was the end for them. And yet every time he was near her he felt the chemistry that had always sizzled between them. That sizzle warned Sutter that they weren't as over as he wanted to believe.

Except the fact that she was at home tonight with her new boyfriend suggested that he might be the only one who felt they weren't over. And that really sucked.

His mother had said that she was making pot roast for dinner, one of his favorites, but he'd declined her invitation to join the family—as he'd declined most of her invitations since returning to Rust Creek Falls. Too much had been said and done for Sutter to pretend otherwise, so aside from working with his father and brothers on the ranch, he usually kept to himself and prepared his own meals at Clay's house. Tonight, he pulled into the parking lot of the Ace in the Hole instead.

He climbed the rough-hewn wooden steps and opened the screen door beneath the oversize playing card—an ace of hearts—that blinked in red neon. The bar was dimly lit and buzzing with conversations that mostly drowned out the Johnny Cash song emanating from the ancient Wurlitzer jukebox that still played three songs for a quarter. A long wooden bar ran the length of one wall and the dozen bar stools that faced the mirrored wall reflecting rows of glass bottles were already occupied, with several other patrons crowded in between the stools and leaned against the bar.

The booths that lined the outer walls were also filled, as were most of the wooden tables that surrounded the small dance floor in the middle of the room. Discarded peanut shells crunched under his boots as he made his way to one of those tables near the mostly unused stage in the far back corner. He pulled out the ladder-back chair and settled onto the creaky seat. The round wooden table was battered and scarred but appeared to be clean.

"What are you doing here?"

Sutter looked up, startled to see Paige's sister Lani standing at his table. She was wearing a pair of jeans and a plaid shirt, so it was only when he saw the apron around her waist and the order pad in her hand that he realized she was his waitress.

And not a very happy one, judging by her tone, so he kept his deliberately light and said, "I was hoping to look at a menu."

She tossed a single laminated page on the table. "That's the menu—look all you want."

"You probably don't get very many tips with an attitude like that," he mused.

"I'll give you a tip—stay away from my sister."

He looked around. "Is Lindsay here, too?"

Lani's eyes narrowed. "You know very well that I'm talking about Paige."

Ellie's roast beef with a side of gentle prying suddenly seemed infinitely more palatable than substandard pub fare with prickly attitude, but no way was he going to let Paige's little sister run him off.

"And I've barely seen her in the three months that I've been back in Rust Creek Falls," he pointed out to her.

"You saw her last night," Lani noted.

"Yeah, and here's a news flash for you—it was a public meeting at town hall."

"You walked her home."

He didn't bother to ask how she knew. This was Rust Creek Falls, where anyone might have seen them and no one could ever keep a secret for very long. "Actually, she would probably say that she was walking alone and I just happened to be beside her."

"Good."

"How about a beer while I try to decide between the cheeseburger and the bacon burger?"

"We're out of bacon."

"In that case, I'll have the cheeseburger and a draft beer."

She nodded and took the menu back, but she didn't move away from his table. "Alex Monroe is a good guy—and he's good to Paige."

"Have I said anything to the contrary?"

"The fact that you're still in Rust Creek Falls says plenty."

"I'm here because I'm helping Collin with his campaign."

"Then you're going back to Seattle after the election?"

"Not that it's any of your business," he felt compelled to point out. "But yes, I'm going back to Seattle after the election."

"And that's why she's better off with Alex," she said triumphantly. "Because he won't leave her."

"But does he love her? And does she love him?"

"She's with him," Lani said firmly. "That's all that should matter to you."

He didn't want to admit she was right, so he only shrugged, as if he was bored by the whole conversation. "Are you going to get my drink now?"

"Maybe." She turned away and went to another table, where a young couple had just sat down. She took their order, immediately returned with their drinks, then went back to the bar again and finally brought Sutter his beer.

The election was in two more days, and then his job here would be over. He should probably hang around a little while longer to tie up any loose ends, but he figured it was safe to assume that he'd be back in Seattle within a week. Back to the freedom and contentment of being anonymous, back to the big city where there weren't memories of Paige Dalton in every direction he turned.

He should forget the burger and get back to the ranch to start packing so he didn't have to spend any more time in Rust Creek Falls than was absolutely necessary. Except that leaving this town meant leaving Paige again, a prospect that was just as unappealing now as it had been five years earlier.

She's better off with Alex.

Sutter suspected that Lani was right, but he wasn't going to believe it was what Paige wanted until he'd heard it directly from her lips.

Paige really liked Alex, but she wasn't in love with him. And while she'd hoped that her feelings for him might grow and deepen with time, as she dished up the peach cobbler she'd made for dessert—using canned fruit in the recipe because there were no fresh peaches to be found in Montana at this time of year—she realized that wasn't likely to happen. At least not so long as Sutter was in Rust Creek Falls.

Not going to think about him, she reminded herself sternly.

The admonishment snapped her attention back to the present but failed to banish all thoughts of the other man from her mind. Which probably wasn't so surprising, considering her extensive history with Sutter. But that was what it was—history. He was her past, and Alex was her future.

Except that she was starting to question whether that was really true. She might want to think she and Alex could have a future, but the more time they spent together, the more difficult it was to imagine they would ever be anything more than friends.

He was an attractive man—objectively she knew this was true—but she wasn't attracted *to* him. Her heart didn't start to pound as soon as she saw him, her blood didn't hum when he was close and her knees didn't go weak when he kissed her. She guessed that Alex probably felt the same way, because he'd never tried to push her for more than the few kisses that they'd shared.

So why had she invited him to dinner tonight? Had she been hoping that he would say or do something to somehow change her mind about their relationship? That he would take her in his arms and kiss her until she was breathless and panting and wanted nothing more than to haul him upstairs to her bed?

As she poked at her dessert, she acknowledged that was what she'd been hoping. And when he'd walked through the door, Alex *had* kissed her. The kiss had been warm and pleasant...and over almost before it began.

"That was a fabulous meal," Alex said, pushing his empty plate aside.

She forced a smile. "I'm glad you were able to make it on such short notice."

"It wasn't a hard decision, considering all that I had waiting at home was a frozen dinner."

"So it was the home cooking and not my company that compelled you to accept my invitation?"

He reached across the table and linked their fingers together. "I always enjoy spending time with you, Paige."

"Why do I feel as if there's a *but* coming?"

His lips curved, but the smile didn't reach his eyes. "But lately I've found myself wondering if there's any hope for a future between us so long as you're still hung up on Sutter Traub."

"I'm not hung up on Sutter," she immediately denied. "In fact, I've barely even seen him since he came back to Rust Creek Falls."

"Because you've been avoiding him," Alex guessed.

She pulled her hand away and stood up to clear the dishes from the table. "Because I don't want to see him."

He followed her into the kitchen. "Why would it matter if you didn't still have feelings for him?"

She hated that he could so easily see a truth that she'd only recently acknowledged to herself. "Our relationship didn't end amicably," she admitted. "So there are probably some unresolved issues."

"Then you need to resolve them," Alex said gently.

"I need to move on with my life."

"You're an incredible woman, Paige. And I've enjoyed the time I've spent with you, but you're never going to move on with your life until you put your history with Sutter behind you."

"It's five years behind me," she protested.

"I stopped by town hall on my way home from work to catch the last part of the debate last night," he told her. "And when you stood up to defend Sutter Traub, there was more passion in your words than in any of the kisses we've ever shared."

She didn't know how to respond to that except to say, "I'm sorry."

"Don't be," he said. "And don't ever settle for less than everything you want."

"You're dumping me, aren't you?"

He shook his head. "I'm letting you go so that you can figure out what you want. If you decide that's me, you know where to find me."

He tucked a strand of hair behind her ear, then lowered his head and touched his lips to hers. It was a nice kiss. Light and friendly, and completely uninspiring. She wanted to feel heat or tingles—*anything*—in response to his touch, but there was nothing.

As she watched Alex drive away, she silently cursed Sutter Traub and the possibility that his kisses had ruined her for any other man.

Chapter Four

Sutter was one of the first voters lined up when the polling station opened on Thursday morning, right behind Collin and Willa, who followed Nathan Crawford. Sutter wouldn't have been surprised to learn that Nate had camped outside of town hall to ensure that he was able to cast the first ballot.

There was a steady stream of voters throughout the day. Some of them wore their allegiance proudly on their lapels in the form of buttons that proclaimed Crawford or Traub, and by Sutter's estimation, they were fairly equal in number—and far outnumbered by the voters who came in grim faced and solemn with no indication as to how they were voting or why.

Nate had several factors in his favor. Aside from his campaign being widely supported and well funded—although no one in town really seemed to know where his money was coming from—he'd lived and worked in Rust Creek Falls his entire life. He was friendly and generally well liked, and he always knew what was going on with everyone in town. Of course, that probably had something to do with the fact that Crawford's General Store was the shopping mecca of Rust Creek Falls and people tended to chat while they browsed, making it the central point of information dissemination, too.

Collin, on the other hand, tended to keep to himself and mind his own business. He lived on Falls Mountain and operated independently out of a renovated workshop on the property. He'd inherited CT Saddles from their great-uncle, Casper Traub, but it was Collin's artistic craftsmanship that had really put the business on the map. He made custom saddles and tack and pretty much anything of leather, and he'd used the same focus and attention to detail that had made the company a success to develop a solid plan to rebuild the town and revitalize the economy.

The polling station closed at 6:00 p.m., at which time Thelma McGee taped up the tops of the boxes and took them into the back room to be counted by the independent vote counters. The first step was to divide the ballots into separate piles: Crawford, Traub and spoiled ballots. Then each pile was counted once, then counted again to double-check the results.

The candidates were entitled to be present during the counting of the ballots, along with an authorized representative. Nate Crawford was there with his campaign manager, Bill Fergus. His parents, his sister, Nina, several close friends and a handful of campaign workers were waiting outside for the results.

Of course, everyone was there in anticipation of a celebration, but only one candidate could win. And Sutter couldn't help but think that if his brother lost, it would be his fault, that he'd tainted Collin's campaign by being part of it. Because he was afraid his family would share that belief, he decided it was somehow less stressful to hide out with Thelma and watch the votes being counted than to wait with his family for the results. So Sutter stayed in the room while Collin opted to remain outside with Willa and the rest of the family, claiming he was too nervous to watch.

It was nearly nine o'clock before the final results

were tallied, and although the numbers were close, when Thelma McGee emerged from the back room it was to announce that Collin Traub was the victor. Of course, Nate Crawford was furious, and although Sutter heard him grumbling and predicting dire consequences for the town, he couldn't dispute the results. For the benefit of the local reporter who was hanging around, he offered Collin a terse congratulations and a brief handshake, then walked out of town hall with his family and supporters trailing after him.

While Collin and Willa and the rest of "Team Traub" were laughing and hugging, Sutter found himself looking around the small gathering of supporters for Paige, but she wasn't there. He knew he had no right to be disappointed. She hadn't made him any promises, but he'd hoped that she would show up anyway. He'd wanted her to share in the victory he was sure wouldn't have happened if not for her words at the town hall meeting earlier in the week.

Her absence was proof to Sutter that she wanted to maintain a certain distance between them, that the brief conversation they'd shared after that meeting hadn't bridged the gap of five years. And maybe that was for the best.

He forgot about Paige—at least for a minute—when he got back to the ranch and discovered that the rest of the family had already gathered there. Bob and Ellie, of course, along with Braden and Dallas and Dallas's three boys—Ryder, Jake and Robbie. Clayton and Antonia had made the trip from Thunder Canyon with their two children, Bennett and Lucy, in tow, as had Forrest and his new wife, Angie.

Ellie had the champagne in the fridge—and sparkling grape juice for the kids and the nursing mother—so that as soon as everyone was gathered, the drinks were ready to be poured. As hugs and kisses were exchanged all around, Bob popped the corks and started the bubbles flowing. It was a joyous celebration—thankfully with enough people around that Sutter could avoid having any direct communication with Forrest.

When the glasses had been distributed, Sutter raised his and called for attention to toast Mayor Collin Traub. Everyone joined in, clinking crystal and adding congratulations and advice, and Forrest leaned over to tap his glass to Sutter's.

It wasn't a big deal—or it shouldn't have been. But to Sutter it was huge. Because in that moment, Forrest had looked him directly in the eye. Not a word had passed between the two of them, but somehow Sutter felt as if the vise that had been squeezing his chest eased, just a little. For the first time in a long time, he actually felt as if he was part of the family, as if he was home.

This is probably a bad idea.

As Paige turned her vehicle into the long drive that led toward the Triple T Ranch, she was seriously questioning the wisdom of her impetuous decision to come here, and yet she couldn't stay away. She'd been pleased to hear about Collin's victory, but her thoughts weren't focused so much on the new mayor as his campaign manager. Which was why she knew this was a bad idea.

And yet she didn't turn her car around; she didn't drive away. Instead, she parked at the end of the long line of vehicles and tried to ignore the pounding of her heart.

She could hear talking and laughing from inside even as she made her way to the door, and she wondered if anyone would be able to hear the ring of the bell over the cacophony of sounds. But her finger had barely lifted from the buzzer when the door was opened and she was face-to-face with Sutter.

"You didn't come to town hall."

She was taken aback by his greeting. Not the accusation of the words so much as the hurt beneath them. She hadn't intended to hurt him. Truthfully, she wouldn't have thought that she could. They were supposed to be beyond that.

But somehow, only two days after vowing to put him out of her mind, she was at his door. And no matter how many times she told herself that she hadn't come to see him, she knew it was a lie.

"I figured I'd already made enough of a public statement at town hall on Monday night."

"Well, you're here now, so you can join the party," he said. Then he pulled her into his embrace and swung her around.

Unable to do anything else, Paige held on as the world spun around her. Even when he released her and her feet were back on solid ground, her head continued to spin. And Paige knew it wasn't a consequence of the physical motion as much as the euphoria of being in Sutter's arms again.

This was definitely a bad idea.

"I'm glad you came."

His smile was so real, his joy so evident, she couldn't help but want to share in the emotion of the moment with him. But that was a dangerous wish, so she said, "I can't stay—I just wanted to congratulate Collin."

The brightness of his smile faded just a little. "Of course," he agreed, and led her to the living room. "Look who decided to join the party."

In response to Sutter's announcement, everyone turned. And Paige realized that every member of the

Traub family was there, including the two brothers who now lived in Thunder Canyon, more than three hundred miles away.

"I apologize for crashing the party," she said, suddenly self-conscious.

"It's not crashing when you were invited," Sutter pointed out to her.

Ellie pressed a glass of champagne into her hand. "It's wonderful to see you, Paige."

The greeting was so warm and sincere that Paige actually felt her throat start to tighten, but she somehow managed to smile. "It's wonderful to see you, too."

Everyone greeted her warmly, if not quite as enthusiastically as Sutter had done. Of course, she'd always gotten on well with his parents and all of his brothers. And when she and Sutter had broken up, she'd missed his family almost as much as she'd missed him.

"Congratulations, Mayor Traub," she said when she'd finally managed to make her way through the crowd to Collin and Willa.

"Thank you," Collin said to her. "And thank you for speaking up at the town hall meeting—you really were the voice of reason in the midst of a lot of emotional chaos."

"I'm not sure that my opinion carried any weight, but I wanted people to focus on the relevant issues."

"It carried a lot of weight," Willa told her. "And swayed a lot of on-the-fence voters."

"Well, now that those votes have been counted, your life is going to get even busier," Paige pointed out.

"We're looking forward to it," Collin said, drawing his new wife closer to his side. "We've got a lot of plans for this town."

"And we're going to need a lot of help to implement

those plans," Willa said, her gaze shifting from Paige to the man standing behind her. "Which is why we're hoping to convince Sutter to stay."

Paige looked up at him, surprised by Willa's admission and wary about his response.

"Plans are for tomorrow," he said lightly. "Tonight is for celebrating."

His response suggested to Paige that his plans hadn't changed. He'd told her that he would be going back to Seattle after the election, and she was counting on that promise. Because contrary to Alex Monroe's parting advice, she didn't want to resolve anything with Sutter—she just wanted him to be gone before he could do any more damage to her fragile heart.

But as she visited with his family, she realized how much she'd missed all of them. She'd always enjoyed spending time with them, and she'd loved his parents as if they were her own. And if anyone was surprised that she'd shown up to take part in the celebration, no one said anything to her. They welcomed her into the fold as easily as they'd always done, almost making her feel as if the past five years had never happened. As if Sutter hadn't broken her heart into a million jagged little pieces.

He reached for her hand, linking their fingers as easily as he'd done a thousand times before. Those thousand times before had been more than five years earlier, but still her pulse skipped and her heart pounded. She wanted to tug her hand away, but she worried that doing so would draw too much attention to the fact that he was holding it.

"I could use some air," he said to her. "Will you take a walk with me?"

She could use some air, too, but going outside with Sutter meant being alone with Sutter, and she wasn't sure that was a good idea. In fact, she was sure it was another bad idea in a day that had already been full of them.

He didn't wait for her response but immediately started tugging her back toward the kitchen. She went with him because it seemed less awkward than refusing. But she was all too conscious of his mother's eyes following as they left the room, and she knew that Ellie was probably speculating as to what it meant.

But it didn't mean anything. Paige wouldn't let it mean anything.

The night was chilly, and she was grateful for the sheepskin-lined denim jacket that she'd worn.

As they walked, Sutter talked excitedly about his brother's plans for the town. She could hear the pride in his voice, and she knew that he was sincerely pleased by Collin's victory.

"It's not going to be an easy job, but I don't doubt he's up to it—especially with Willa by his side."

"They're obviously both committed to the rebuilding of Rust Creek Falls," she agreed.

"And to each other," Sutter noted. "It makes a world of difference to know that someone has your back, no matter what problems might arise."

"She loves him," Paige said simply.

"You used to have my back—I don't think I really appreciated that at the time. I don't think I ever realized how much I needed your support until you weren't there anymore."

"I was still there," she felt compelled to point out. "You were the one who left."

"You're right," he admitted. "But that didn't stop me from missing you."

"I agreed to take a walk, not a stroll down memory lane."

"If the past is really the past, why are you so afraid to talk about it?"

She was afraid because she knew how dangerous it could be to talk about the past, to remember how things used to be, how good she and Sutter had been together.

"I just prefer to look forward rather than back," she told him.

"That's too bad, because I have some really fond memories of the time I spent with you."

"It's starting to snow."

"What?" He looked up, and seemed startled by the thick white flakes that were falling down around them.

She'd been surprised by the change in the weather, too, focused so intently on Sutter that she hadn't been aware of anything else. In fact, she hadn't even noticed the snow until she saw the white flakes against his dark jacket and in his thick hair.

"We should get back," she said now and turned toward the house.

Sutter caught her hand again. "You used to like walking in the snow, and I'm not ready to let go of you just yet."

He'd had no such qualms five years ago—not just letting her go, but moving more than five hundred miles away. But she didn't say any of that aloud. She didn't want him to know how much his decision had hurt, how much it still hurt.

"Do you remember the first night I kissed you?"

Of course she remembered. She remembered every little detail of that night despite the eleven years that had passed since then.

"It was a snowy night much like tonight," he continued when she failed to respond to his question. "After the high school Christmas concert.

"You were in the choir and I was in the audience, and when I looked up at you on stage—you took my breath away. I don't know if it was the song you were singing or the white robe you were wearing, but you looked just like an angel.

"And when you stepped forward to sing your solo in 'Silent Night'… I've never heard anything more beautiful. Before or after. And when the concert was finally over and everyone was starting to file out of the auditorium, I asked if I could walk you home."

He'd stuttered a little over the words, as if he was nervous. She'd been just as nervous—maybe even more so. And though her parents had been in the audience and were waiting to give her a ride home, she'd opted to walk with Sutter. She'd been just sixteen years old, and totally infatuated with him.

"I held your hand," he reminded her, then smiled. "And I remember thinking it was a good thing we were both wearing gloves, because my palms were clammy. I think I fell a little bit in love with you that night, and I was as terrified as I was excited that you'd agreed to walk with me.

"It was cold enough that we could see our breath in the air, and the snow crunched beneath our feet as we walked, but I didn't feel cold. Because with every step of the five blocks from the high school to your parents' house, all I could think about was how much I wanted to kiss you, and whether or not you would let me."

He stopped now and tipped her face up, forcing her to meet his gaze. "Do you remember any of that?"

"I remember that it was cold," she told him. "And that my fingers and toes were numb even before we got to the church."

His brows drew together. "*That's* what you remember?"

She heard the disappointment in his tone and her heart softened. "And when we got to my house, we stood behind the stand of lodgepole pines," she continued, "out of sight of anyone peering through the windows, and you kissed me."

He'd slipped his arms around her, drawing her close. Her heart had pounded; her knees had gone weak. His eyes had held hers as his head lowered slowly, until his lips brushed against hers.

Her heart was pounding and the nerves in her belly were jangling as he drew her into his arms now. She couldn't claim she didn't know what he was planning to do any more than she could claim she didn't want his kiss. When his mouth touched hers, the line between the past and present blurred. As the snowflakes swirled around them, Paige could almost believe she was sixteen again. Certainly her heart was pounding as hard and fast as it had then.

His tongue stroked the seam of her lips, a silent entreaty that she couldn't refuse. Her lips parted on a sigh, welcoming him. As the kiss deepened, she knew that this wasn't a memory. Because Sutter's kiss was that of a man, not a boy. And the innocent curiosity she'd felt as a teenage girl had been replaced by a woman's yearning.

His arms tightened around her so that they were pressed together from shoulder to thigh. Despite the thick coats they both wore, she could feel the heat emanating from his body and the answering fire that pumped through her veins. He was hot and hard—yeah, there was no mistaking the evidence of his arousal when he was pressed against her—and she wanted him just as much as he wanted her.

Do we need to make an itemized list of all the reasons that this was a bad idea?

The taunting voice of her subconscious made her pull away. But she kept her hands on his arms, holding on to him, because she wasn't entirely sure that her legs would support her. She drew in a deep breath and willed her heart to settle back inside of her chest.

She was undeniably shaken by the intensity of their kiss. Whatever she'd anticipated when she'd agreed to walk with Sutter, it wasn't this. She couldn't do this—she wouldn't get wrapped up in Sutter Traub again, especially when she knew his return to Rust Creek Falls was only temporary.

When she was sure that her legs would support her, she took a careful step back. "It's late, and I need to get home."

As she turned, Sutter said, "Who's running away now?"

She didn't respond. Because she couldn't deny that she *was* running, but she had a valid reason: he'd already broken her heart once and she wasn't going to let him do it again.

Chapter Five

Sutter held his ground as he watched her retreat, because he knew that if he chased after her, he might very well beg. And he'd never been the type to beg. So he watched her go as his own wants and needs continued to churn inside of him.

Kissing Paige Dalton was not the smartest thing he'd ever done. On the other hand, he knew it had been inevitable, that they had been moving inexorably toward this moment since he'd walked her home from the town hall debate earlier in the week.

He'd wanted one kiss—just to prove to himself that she didn't have the same hold on him that she used to. Except that one kiss had proved him wrong. She tasted just like he remembered—right down to the cherry lip balm she'd favored when she was sixteen. Just one kiss and he knew that he wanted her as much now as he had then. Maybe even more, because he knew how good they were together.

Except that Paige was with someone else now—a fact that he'd conveniently forgotten when he'd had her in his arms. He figured it was a safe bet that she'd forgotten about the mill foreman, too. There was no way she'd been thinking about another man while she'd been kissing him.

But one kiss didn't change the fact that she had a life without him. Or that her life was here in Rust Creek Falls and his was in Seattle.

And he liked his life in Washington. He was proud of the business he'd built and the success it had become. He'd made new friends and he never lacked for female companionship if he wanted it. But he'd missed his family and his friends in Montana. And he'd missed Paige.

He'd dated a lot of women in the past five years, trying to forget about her. Because he'd been certain that he would eventually meet someone who would make him forget the first woman he'd ever loved. The only woman he'd ever loved. Now, five years later, he was starting to wonder if she might be the only woman for him.

When he'd left town, he'd been full of hurt and anger, determined to prove to himself and everyone else that he didn't need anything or anyone he'd left behind. With time and distance, his indignation had eventually faded. He'd accepted that his own actions might have been a bit impulsive and not completely rational. But he still hadn't been willing to admit he'd made a mistake, and he hadn't been ready to go home. He'd left Rust Creek Falls with the intention of proving that he could make it on his own, and it had taken a while, but he'd done so. He'd built a successful business for himself in Seattle. He had a nice home and a comfortable life.

And truthfully, for the first year after he'd opened the doors of his stables, he hadn't had time for anything else. But lately he'd begun to feel that something was missing. When he went home to an empty house at the end of the day, he considered that it might be nice to have some company—and for more than just a few hours. In fact, it might be nice to share his life with someone.

Except that he hadn't met anyone in Seattle who inspired him to think of long-term plans. He'd met a lot of attractive, intelligent and fascinating women, but he couldn't imagine spending the rest of his life with any one of them. Because when he'd been barely twenty years old and head over heels in love with Paige Dalton, they'd made plans for their future together. Obviously things hadn't turned out the way they'd planned, but he couldn't forget the dreams they'd shared—and he couldn't imagine any other woman occupying the space she still held in his heart.

When Paige's taillights disappeared at the end of the long drive, he finally headed back toward the house and the party still going on inside.

"Everything okay?" Collin asked when he returned.

"Everything's fine."

"Good, because I wanted to talk to you about some of the ideas Lissa Roarke had to generate national interest in the rebuild of Rust Creek Falls."

"I was your campaign manager. The campaign is over," Sutter pointed out to him. "You don't need my advice or opinion on anything anymore."

"I need your help."

He shook his head. "I'm sure Lissa has everything under control, and I have to get back to Seattle."

"You're really going to leave?"

"That was always the plan," Sutter reminded him.

"I know," his brother admitted. "But I thought—I hoped—things had changed."

His mind drifted back to the kiss he'd shared with Paige. That all-too-brief moment had proved to Sutter that his feelings for her were as strong and steadfast as ever.

"No," he said. "Nothing has changed."

Ellie Traub couldn't sleep. And when she couldn't sleep, she ended up tossing and turning, disturbing Bob's sleep. The alternative was to slip out of bed and pace. When the boys were younger, Bob used to tease that she was going to wear out the floor by the window. She'd put an area rug on the floor—not really to protect the wood but to muffle her steps so that he wouldn't hear her.

She'd paced for each and every one of her boys on numerous occasions, some more than others. She'd done a lot of pacing when Forrest was in Iraq. It was the hardest thing in the world for a mother to know that her child was in danger and not be able to do anything to help. When he came home wounded, she only cared that he was home. Yes, he had scars—physical and emotional—but he was alive and the healing could begin.

She'd hoped that Sutter might come home then, too. She hadn't realized how deeply he'd been wounded by the falling-out with Forrest and, consequently, the rest of the family. But he'd come home when he'd heard about the floods because he'd known the family needed him, and that gave her hope that he might someday come home to stay for good. Seeing him with Paige Dalton tonight further bolstered that hope.

Ellie had always liked the young schoolteacher. Even when Paige and Sutter were in high school together, she'd thought that they were well suited. Paige had spent a lot of time at the Triple T back then—so much that Ellie had begun to think of her as part of the family. In fact, she'd been certain that Paige would be her daughter-in-law someday. And then Sutter had left town and broken Paige's heart.

She'd come to the ranch tonight—ostensibly to congratulate Collin, but Ellie hadn't missed the looks that had passed between Paige and Sutter, or the crackle in the air whenever they stood close to one another. Whatever had been between them clearly wasn't over—but was it enough to keep her son in Rust Creek Falls?

"I thought that once the election was over you'd stop pacing the bedroom floor at midnight," Bob said.

Ellie froze. "I'm sorry if I woke you."

"Why don't you tell me what's on your mind?"

Because it was obvious that something was, she replied without hesitation, "Sutter."

"You're worried that he's going to go back to Seattle now," he guessed, shifting so that he was sitting up in bed, leaning back against the headboard.

She nodded.

"He's a grown man—he has to make his own choices."

"I understand why he left—and I know we bear some responsibility for that, for letting him think that our decision to support Forrest meant we didn't support him. But I didn't think he'd stay away for so long."

"He's built a life and a career for himself in Seattle."

She lowered herself onto the edge of the mattress. "I want him to come home."

"He came home when we needed him," Bob pointed out.

"I want him to stay," she insisted stubbornly.

He lifted a hand and gently brushed her hair away from her face. "I want that, too, but it's what Sutter wants that matters."

"I think he'd stay this time, if Paige asked him to."

Bob sighed. "Ellie."

"I know she's been dating the mill foreman, but even a blind person could see that there are still sparks between her and Sutter."

"I know you like Paige and that you'd like nothing better for them to get back together, but you have to let them live their own lives."

"Did you see them together tonight?"

"Yes, I saw them. But they're not together anymore," he reminded her.

"He still loves her."

"Did he tell you that?"

"As if he would."

"Then let it be," he suggested.

She folded her arms over her chest.

He smiled and leaned forward to brush his lips against hers. "I love you, Ellie."

Even now, after forty years of marriage, his kiss warmed her inside. And when he eased her back onto the mattress, she didn't protest.

"I love you, too," she told him. "And I love the life we have together, so why is it wrong to want the same happiness for my children?"

He settled her head onto his shoulder and held her close. "It's not wrong to want it—it's only wrong if you try to manipulate it."

She sighed softly. "I'm not trying to manipulate, just to…nurture the possibility."

"Right now, you should try to go to sleep," he suggested.

She closed her eyes and followed his advice.

The flowers confused her.

Paige scowled at the gorgeous bouquet of yellow and orange gerbera daisies on her dining room table and tried to figure out what they were supposed to mean. Not their symbolic meaning, but why Sutter had sent them. The brief message on the card—"Thanks for always having my back, S."—was an echo of what he'd said to her the night before, so the flowers were redundant. Beautiful but redundant.

So why had he sent them? Was it because of the kiss? It

had been one kiss—a simple and inconsequential meeting of their lips. Okay, the fact that she'd tossed and turned through most of the night suggested that it might not have been quite as inconsequential as she wanted to believe. Still, it was only one kiss.

But it was a kiss that made her want more.

She turned her back on the flowers and returned to the lesson she'd been teaching before the ring of the bell had interrupted. Of course, she should have realized that the delivery would not go unnoticed. And she should have expected that her class of fifth graders would be more interested in the flowers than the chapter of the book she'd instructed them to read and summarize.

As soon as she returned to the living room and asked if there were any questions, Allyson's hand shot into the air.

"Who are the flowers from?"

"A friend," she said, because it seemed the simplest if not necessarily the most accurate response.

"Your boyfriend?" Emma asked, not bothering to put her hand in the air.

"No, just a friend."

"A boy friend or a girl friend?" Becky wanted to know.

Paige drew in a breath and mentally counted to ten. "Let's forget about the flowers and concentrate on chapter three for the next twenty minutes," she suggested. "Now, who can tell me what it was about mules that made them ideal for working in the coal mines?"

David, one of the more focused students in her class, raised his hand. "Because they were sure-footed and strong."

"That's right," she agreed. "Anything else?"

His attention dropped back to the book, and his classmates followed suit, looking for the answers to her questions in the passage they'd read.

Paige exhaled slowly, confident that her students were back on track.

The rest of the day went fairly smoothly—until her sisters stopped by after dinner.

Paige was just washing up the dishes when she heard the cursory knock at the back door before Lani and Lindsay walked in.

"Mom sent leftover meat loaf," Lindsay said.

"Thanks." Paige took the container from her sister and put it in the fridge. There was no point in reminding her mother that she'd been living on her own for almost two years now—it wouldn't stop Mary from sending food, just like her repeated assertion that she didn't like meat loaf hadn't stopped her mother from trying to get her to eat it.

"Is that the only reason you stopped by—to perform your assigned meals-on-wheels duty?"

"No. We're actually heading out for movie night and thought you might want to come with us," Lani told her.

There wasn't an actual movie theater in Rust Creek Falls, but every Friday night was movie night in the high school auditorium. Of course, they were never new releases. Sometimes they were recent movies, but more often they were classic films or family favorites.

"What's playing?"

Lani named the film, and although it was one of Paige's favorites, she shook her head. "I've seen it at least a dozen times."

Lindsay shrugged. "So have we, but it happens to be what's playing tonight."

"I'd rather stay home and mark spelling tests." She folded her towel and draped it over the handle of the oven.

When she moved away, Lani spotted the flowers.

"Well, well… Does this mean you've finally taken

your relationship with Alex to the next level?" she teased her sister.

"Only you would equate a simple bunch of flowers with sex."

"Actually, I'd hope for something a little fancier than daisies after sex."

Lindsay frowned at the bouquet. "Didn't Sutter always give you gerberas?"

He had, because he knew that they were Paige's favorites. Not as elegant as lilies or as fancy as roses, but simple and beautiful.

Before she could say anything, Lani reached forward to snag the card that she'd tucked in with the blooms, and Paige silently cursed herself for not tearing it into pieces and tossing it into the trash.

"These are from Sutter," she said accusingly, then turned to Paige, her hands fisted on her hips. "Why is Sutter Traub sending you flowers?"

"I don't know," Paige insisted, though the guilty flush that swept her cheeks certainly suggested otherwise. "Maybe because I told him that I would vote for Collin and Collin won the election."

"I voted for Collin, too," Lindsay said. "I didn't get any flowers."

"So did I," Lani noted. "And I don't believe for a minute that the new mayor's brother sent flowers to thank you for marking an X on a ballot, so spill."

"There's nothing to spill," Paige said.

"We're your sisters." Lindsay's tone was more persuasive than demanding. "You can tell us anything."

"If there was anything to tell, I would," Paige assured her. "But there is nothing to tell."

"How about the fact that you were at the Triple T last night?" Lani challenged.

She frowned. "How do you know that?"

"I saw Ellie at the library this afternoon, and she commented about how pleased she was that you went by to congratulate Collin last night."

"Yes, I went to the Triple T to congratulate Collin last night."

"And of course Sutter, as Collin's campaign manager, would have been there, too," Lani noted.

"Yes," she said again. "Sutter was there."

"And?" Lindsay prompted.

"And we talked a little—mostly about Collin's plans for Rust Creek Falls."

"Mostly," Lani said, zeroing in on that single word. "Which means that you talked about other things, too."

Paige sighed. "The weather, because it was cold and starting to snow."

"Just like the first night Sutter kissed you, when you were in high school," Lindsay remembered.

She rolled her eyes. "And you wonder why I don't tell you anything?"

"So there is something you aren't telling us," Lani decided.

"You don't have to tell us," Lindsay said. "But it's obvious that Sutter has somehow managed to get under your skin again."

"He hasn't," she denied, though not very convincingly.

Lindsay touched her hand. "You were in love with him once," she reminded her gently.

Paige just nodded.

"And he stomped all over your heart," Lani said, her tone not at all gentle.

"Thanks for the reminder," Paige said drily. "I'd almost forgotten that part."

"Sorry," Lani said, not sounding sorry at all. "I just

want to make sure you don't forget—and that you don't give him a chance to do it again."

"No worries there," Paige assured her. "Now that the election's over, I don't think he'll be hanging around Rust Creek Falls too much longer."

Lindsay cast another worried glance at the vase filled with flowers. "I wouldn't be so sure."

"Why do you say that?" Lani demanded.

"Because I can and do hate Sutter for what he did to Paige, but he was never the type of guy to play fast and loose with a girl's heart. These flowers—*Paige's favorite flowers*—make me think that he's not over our big sister."

"I don't care if he is or isn't, as long as he goes back to Seattle," Lani said.

"I appreciate your concern," Paige said to her sisters. "But there's really no need for it. My heart is completely Sutter proofed now."

Even if Sutter had heard Paige's proclamation, he wouldn't have been dissuaded. And he wouldn't have believed it, anyway. Because when they'd kissed the night before, he'd felt the connection, as strong and undeniable as it had been five years earlier.

And that was why he was at her door at eight o'clock on Friday night. He'd tried calling first—in fact, he'd called several times during the day. He knew that she was home because she was teaching, and he could understand why she wouldn't want to interrupt a lesson to answer the phone. Still, he didn't understand why she hadn't found five minutes in the several hours that had passed since her students went home to return his call.

He knew it was possible—even probable—that she might be out with Alex Monroe. Or that he might be at her house again. It was a chance he was willing to take.

He wasn't willing to let Paige pretend he didn't exist any longer. But he was relieved when he saw that only her car was in the driveway.

She opened the door in response to his knock, but she didn't look happy to see him.

"What are you doing here, Sutter?"

He held up the plastic-wrapped plate. "I brought celebration cake."

She eyed the plate warily. "Why?"

"Because my mom's cheesecake used to be your favorite."

The wariness was replaced by interest. "That's your mom's mile-high cherry cheesecake?"

"As if I would show up here with any kind of imitation."

"Are you going to hand it over or do I have to invite you inside?"

"An invitation would be nice," he told her.

She stepped away from the door.

"And a cup of coffee would be even nicer."

"Would you like a cup of coffee?"

"How could I possibly say no to such a gracious offer?"

Her lips curved just a little as she led the way to the kitchen.

He glanced around the room, noted the glossy white cabinets, deep blue backsplash, granite countertops and stainless-steel appliances. Instead of a kitchen table there was an island, with four stools set up in counter-style seating. He spotted the bouquet of daisies tucked in the back corner of the counter by the refrigerator.

"I see you got the flowers."

"They're beautiful," she acknowledged with more than a hint of reluctance in her tone. "But they really weren't necessary."

"I know they weren't necessary, but I wanted to give you flowers."

"Why?" She measured out coffee grounds, dumped them into the paper filter.

"Do I need a reason?"

She poured water into the reservoir. "You need to understand that what happened last night shouldn't have happened, and that it won't happen again."

He smiled. "'What happened last night' makes it sound like it was a much bigger thing than it was."

"It wasn't a big thing at all—it was just a kiss."

"So why are you so bent out of shape over a bunch of daisies?"

"I'm not," she immediately denied, then huffed out a breath. "Okay, maybe I am."

"Then maybe you need to figure out why."

"Because our relationship was over five years ago. Because the flowers were delivered while I was in the middle of a lesson with my class. Because my sisters were here earlier and demanded to know why you were sending me flowers." She ticked the reasons off on her fingers as she enumerated them, then she looked at him. "I think any of those reasons would suffice, so pick one."

Sutter winced. "I didn't think about the fact that your students would be here." He looked around. "Where do you put them?"

"Not in here," she admitted. "I have sixteen if they all show up."

"If?" he prompted.

"Attendance has been a bit of a problem since the flood," she told him. "Some parents don't seem to understand that I'm following the curriculum—teaching essential subjects to their kids so they're not behind when we do get back into a real classroom. They seem to think that because this isn't actually a school, attendance is optional."

"So where is the classroom?"

She opened a pair of French doors and led him into the living room, where her furniture—a butter-yellow sofa, two matching armchairs with ottomans and a set of glass-and-metal occasional tables—had all been pushed back against the walls to make room for the long folding tables and chairs that occupied the middle of the room.

"And you spend the whole day in here with sixteen kids?"

She laughed softly. "You're feeling claustrophobic just thinking about it, aren't you?"

"A little," he admitted, not surprised that she'd read his thoughts so easily. No one had ever understood him like Paige. In fact, when he'd first told her about his job interview at a management company in Seattle, she'd warned that he wouldn't last behind a desk, that he'd go crazy stuck in an office.

"Actually, I try not to keep them cooped up in here all day. If the weather's nice, I walk them down the street to the Country Kids Day Care so they can run around outside—that's our physical education component. And if there's research to be done, we go over to the library to use the computers there."

The coffeepot hissed, signaling that it was finished brewing. Paige turned back to the kitchen and poured two mugs of coffee. He took the one she handed to him, shook his head when she offered cream and sugar. He'd always taken his coffee black, and he saw that she still did, too.

He settled onto one of the stools at the island while Paige cut the slice of cheesecake down the middle, then transferred one half to a second plate. She carried the plates and forks to the island, but instead of sitting beside him, she remained standing on the opposite side.

She cut off a piece of cake, then slid the fork between her lips. Her eyelids closed and a sound of pleasure hummed in her throat. "Mmm. This is even more incredible than I remembered."

The expression on her face was pure bliss—a both tempting and painful reminder that she was a sensual woman who enjoyed indulging in all kinds of pleasures.

"Ellie Traub's secret recipe," he said lightly. "She doesn't let anyone step foot in the kitchen while she's making it."

"She let me help her with it once."

"She did not."

"She did," Paige insisted. "She was making it for the baby shower, when Laurel was pregnant with Robbie."

"Mom always did like you best," he said, managing to coax another smile from her.

She polished off the last of her cake, then picked up her mug of coffee and sipped.

"Do you want me to apologize for the flowers?" he asked.

She glanced at the colorful blossoms and sighed softly. "No. I don't want you to apologize."

"What do you want?"

"I want you to go back to Seattle." She looked at him now, her gaze steady and sure. "I *need* you to go back to Seattle."

Chapter Six

Paige saw the disappointment and hurt on his face, but she didn't—couldn't—let herself be swayed by emotion. He'd asked what she wanted, and she wasn't going to feel guilty about giving him an honest answer.

Except that deep in her heart, she knew that it wasn't an honest answer. She didn't want Sutter to go back to Seattle—she wanted him to stay in Rust Creek Falls forever. But she knew that wasn't an option, so the next best thing was for him to leave as soon as possible before she started wishing for things she knew she couldn't have.

"Because you're afraid of what might happen between us if I stay," he guessed.

Paige didn't know what irritated her more—the cockiness of his tone or the fact that he was right. Of course, she had no intention of admitting as much.

"Nothing's going to happen between us," she told him in her firmest teacher voice.

"Something already happened," he reminded her.

"You kissed me," she acknowledged in a deliberately casual tone. "It wasn't a big deal."

"I might have started it, but you kissed back pretty good," he pointed out. "In fact, I'd say a lot better than pretty good. And it was a big deal."

She felt her cheeks flush. "I did kiss you back, and I shouldn't have."

"Because you feel guilty about Alex?"

It was an easy excuse, and preferable to the truth—which was that one kiss from Sutter had made her want a lot more kisses, a lot more touching, a lot more everything. And that was a dangerous way of thinking.

"No," she admitted. "Alex and I aren't seeing one another anymore. But that doesn't change the fact that I have no intention of starting something with you again."

"I'd say it's already started," he told her.

She shook her head.

"Are you really trying to deny the chemistry between us?"

"We didn't break up because of a lack of chemistry," she reminded him.

"You're right," he admitted. "But the more time I spend with you, the more difficult it is to remember why we did break up."

"Because you were determined to get out of Rust Creek Falls and I didn't want to leave. And that hasn't changed."

"Maybe it has," he said. "Why won't you at least give us a chance?"

She shook her head again.

"I'm not the same man I was five years ago," he told her. "And I'm not going to walk away from what I want this time."

"Whether you stay or go is your choice—but don't make the mistake of thinking it has anything to do with me."

"If I stay, will you go out with me?"

"No."

"I'm not asking you to make any life-altering decisions, I'm just asking you to spend some time with me."

She picked up the empty plates and carried them to the sink. She refused to let herself even think about his invitation. No good would come from spending time with Sutter—and despite her assurance to her sisters, she knew that her heart wasn't nearly as Sutter proof as she wanted to believe. In fact, it was already softening as her resolve was weakening.

"Just one date," he cajoled. "And if you don't have a good time with me, I'll back off."

"Really?"

"Really," he assured her.

"Just one date?" she asked, still skeptical.

"One date. Whatever you want to do."

Paige considered for another minute, her common sense warring with her curiosity. And in the back of her mind, it occurred to her that if he was offering to do anything she wanted, she really could use his help with something. She finally nodded. "Okay."

"How does tomorrow night sound?"

She shook her head. "Tomorrow morning. Early."

"How early?"

"You can pick me up at eight."

Sutter suspected that his Saturday-morning date with Paige was going to be unlike any other date he'd ever experienced. His first clue was the hour—obviously she wasn't planning a candlelit dinner and romantic movie, but he didn't care. All that mattered was that he would get to spend time with Paige. But as he made his way into town Saturday morning, it occurred to him that the only time he'd been at a woman's house at eight in the morning was when he'd spent the night before in her bed.

Unfortunately, he hadn't spent Friday night in Paige's bed. But he did pick up breakfast for both of them—if donuts and coffee from Daisy's Donuts could be considered breakfast. Since she hadn't told him what their plan was for the day, he'd dressed casually in a pair of jeans and a flannel shirt with his favorite leather jacket. He'd nicked his jaw when he was shaving, so he double-checked his face in the rearview mirror to make sure he didn't have any tissue stuck to the cut before he exited the vehicle.

She met him at the door, obviously eager to get going—wherever it was they were going. She was dressed just as casually in jeans, a zip-up hoodie and jean jacket. But he couldn't help but notice how the softly faded jeans molded to the sweet curve of her buttocks, or how the layers she wore on top emphasized the slenderness of her frame. She had running shoes on her feet and her long dark hair was pulled back into a ponytail.

Aside from the simple silver hoops that hung from her ears and the pink gloss on her lips, she wore no decorations or makeup. Of course, Paige had the kind of natural beauty that didn't require any artificial enhancement. She looked young and fresh and as beautiful as always. And when she smiled at him, his heart actually ached.

"You made it." Her eyes lit on the paper cup holder in his hand and her smile widened. "And you brought coffee?"

"And donuts," he told her.

"What kind?"

"Powdered sugar with lemon filling."

She reached for the bag. "It's not fair that you know all my weaknesses."

"And some much more interesting ones than cheesecake and powdered-sugar donuts."

"One date," she reminded him, pulling a donut out of the bag. "And then you're going to back off."

She sounded so optimistic he might have been insulted if he didn't believe that her desperation to get him out of her life was a reflection of the depth of her feelings for him. "I will back off," he agreed. "If you don't have a good time."

She bit into the donut. "The fact that I'm going to enjoy this doesn't count."

"Okay, the good-time register doesn't start until the coffee and donuts are done and we're at… Where are we going?"

"To the elementary school."

"Isn't it still under repair?"

"Yep." Her lips curved, just a little. "You know how to swing a hammer, cowboy?"

"I think I can figure it out."

The repair of the school was coming along slowly but surely. The first part—tearing out everything that had been damaged by the flood—had been completed fairly quickly thanks to the large number of residents who had volunteered to help out. The second part—rebuilding what had been destroyed—was a bigger task, and a more costly one. Numerous delays had held up the work, mostly resulting from a lack of funding.

The school board's insurance company was dragging its feet, insisting that more information was needed before it could settle the claim. Of course, without money there wasn't a lot that could be done. Some supplies had been donated, and a small fund had been collected from residents to help with the rebuild.

But the reality was that almost every family in Rust Creek Falls had been affected by the flood, and while everyone wanted to help, most were in the same predicament, with their time and resources stretched too thin to be able to stretch any further. Even the generous donation that Lissa Roarke, a transplanted Manhattanite now engaged to Gage Christensen, had procured from a New York–based nonprofit organization called Bootstraps hadn't been enough to finance the project.

So Paige was more than a little surprised when they arrived and found twice the usual number of volunteers and every one of them busy at work. The site was buzzing, not just with activity but with information. Apparently Lissa had recently appeared on a national morning show to discuss the plight of Rust Creek Falls, and the result had been an unexpected influx of both monetary donations and building supplies. Having funds and materials made a huge difference, and of course the townspeople had done the rest, volunteering their time and labor. Those who couldn't provide physical labor brought other things to the table—literally.

A handful of picnic tables had been set up on the property and from noon until about two o'clock, there were platters of sandwiches and a steady supply of Crock-Pots filled with hot soups and stews to fuel the workers. There were also plates of cookies, bowls of fruit and vats of coffee.

Paige and Sutter focused their efforts on her fifth-grade classroom. They worked with Dean and Nick Pritchett, who expertly measured, cut and installed the last of the drywall, following behind to tape and mud the seams and nails. Of course, Dean and Nick were finished long before Paige and Sutter, leaving the two of them working alone together for most of the afternoon.

"Is this how you spend every Saturday?"

"For the past few weeks," she admitted. "For a long time there wasn't anything to do because we were stuck waiting for permits and funding. Considering that, it's amazing how much progress has been made in such a short time."

"Are all of the teachers here?"

"Not just teachers, but support and admin staff, parents and a lot of citizens who have no direct interest in the school and their own work to do. It's the way that towns like Rust Creek Falls work."

"I haven't been gone that long," he noted drily.

"I know," she admitted. But at times it had felt like forever. "And I know life in the big city hasn't changed you too much."

"How do you know that?"

"Because you came all the way from Seattle when you heard about the flood."

"It isn't all that far."

But she knew that it was. More than five hundred miles, and there were times she felt as if it might as well have been five thousand because of the distance the move put between her and Sutter.

"Well, I know it meant a lot to your family, that you came home." She leaned over and touched her lips to his cheek. "And it meant a lot to me that you were willing to help out here today."

When she started to draw back, he slipped his arm around her waist and held her close. "I was willing to do anything, so long as it meant spending some time with you."

"Why?"

"Because I miss you. I didn't even realize how much until I came home and saw you again."

She'd missed him, too, which was exactly why she didn't want to go down the same path again. "Spending time together is only going to make it harder when you leave again."

"But you had a good time today, didn't you?"

"I feel good about what we accomplished here," she allowed.

"C'mon, Paige. Just admit you had a good time."

"I had a good time."

"Me, too," he said, and smiled as he lowered his head toward her.

She lifted her hands to his chest. "What are you doing?"

"You kissed me," he said. "Now it's my turn to kiss you."

"It was just to thank you for helping out today."

His mouth hovered just a fraction of an inch above hers. "Then you can consider this a thank-you for letting me help out," he said, and captured her lips.

Paige knew she should pull away, because letting Sutter kiss her again was a tried-and-true recipe for heartbreak. But as soon as his mouth touched hers, all thoughts of resistance were forgotten. In that first moment of contact, she couldn't seem to focus on any of the dozens of reasons that this was a bad idea. She could only think that this was exactly what she wanted.

Her eyes drifted shut; her body swayed toward him. His hands slid up her back, drawing her closer. He tilted her head back, deepened the kiss. The hands she'd lifted to hold him at a distance slid over his shoulders to toy with the soft, silky strands of hair that touched his collar.

He touched the tip of his tongue to her lips, delved inside when they parted for him. Her arms had wrapped around him and her breasts were crushed against his chest, her hips aligned with his. Despite the layers of clothes between them, she could feel the heat of his body, the imprint of his hands, the press of his erection. Heat rushed through her veins, pooled low in her belly.

There was definitely chemistry between them.

Very potent chemistry.

But as she'd reminded him the night of the election,

the attraction between them had never been the issue. Right now, in the comfort of his arms, she had trouble remembering what the issue had been. What had come between them? And why had she ever let him go?

When he finally eased his lips from hers, they were both breathless. After a moment, he said, "Now that makes it official."

She realized that she was still in his arms, her cheek resting against the warm flannel of his shirt so that she could feel the steady beat of his heart. She forced herself to take a step back. "Makes what official?"

"It's not really a date unless it ends with a kiss," he told her.

It was the perfect excuse to say goodbye and find her own way home. They'd spent the day together working at the school—not a traditional date by any stretch of the imagination, but he had allowed her to choose the venue—and now it was over.

And yet she heard herself say, "If our date is ended, does that mean you're not going to buy me dinner?"

He seemed just as surprised as she was by the words that came out of her mouth, but he recovered quickly. "I'll buy you dinner," he agreed readily. "But I think I'm going to need a shower first."

She glanced down at her mud-spattered clothes. "Me, too."

"You know, it would conserve water if we took that shower together," he suggested.

She shook her head. "Your environmental consciousness is impressive, but I don't see that happening."

He just grinned. "Can't blame a guy for trying."

Paige had just stripped out of her clothes when there was a knock on the door. Thinking that Sutter had forgotten something—or was pretending that he'd forgotten something in the hope of catching her half-dressed—she hastily tugged on her robe and went to the door.

"Yes, I believe in conserving..." The words faded away when she realized it wasn't Sutter on her porch but her middle brother. "Oh, Travis. Hi."

His brows drew together as his gaze skimmed over the robe. "You were expecting someone else?"

She sighed and stepped away from the door. "I wasn't expecting anyone. Sutter just left and—"

"So that *was* him—the guy you were with at the school?"

"Yes, we were both at the school." She went to the fridge and pulled out a bottle of the beer that she kept on hand for whenever one of her brothers visited—which they rarely did.

Anderson, Travis and Caleb were all busy with their own lives, but she knew that they were never far away. And though she didn't often call on them for help, it was comforting to know that they were close if she needed anything.

Her brother's scowl deepened as he twisted the cap off the bottle. "Why was he there?"

"Because we need all the help we can get if we have any hope of getting the kids back into that building for the beginning of the new year," she reminded him. "Why are *you* here?"

He straddled one of the stools at the island. "I ran into Nate as I was fueling up at the gas station."

"And that was so noteworthy you had to stop by to tell me about it?" Since it seemed as if her brother was settling in, she considered pulling another beer out of the fridge for herself. Except that she was going to be seeing Sutter again in a while, and the last thing she needed was to have her ability to think clearly compromised by alcohol, especially when just being near Sutter tended to cloud her mind.

"I stopped by because he happened to mention that he'd seen you with Sutter Traub."

She doubted he had just happened to mention it—knowing Nate Crawford, it was more likely he'd deliberately tattled to her big brother. "So?"

He frowned at her response. "You're not denying it?"

She leaned back against the counter and folded her arms across her chest. "Rust Creek Falls is hardly a booming metropolis. As long as Sutter's in town our paths are going to cross, and I don't have to explain my actions to anyone—not to you and certainly not to Nate Crawford."

"What about to Alex Monroe?"

"My relationship with Alex isn't any of your business, either," she told him. "But if it was, I would tell you that we aren't seeing each other anymore."

"Because of Sutter?"

"Because our relationship wasn't going anywhere."

"I always liked Sutter, but I don't want you to get hurt again," Travis said sincerely.

"I don't want that either, but I'm not going to cut Sutter out of my life just because we have a history."

"It's not the history that worries me but the present," he said.

"You don't need to worry at all," she assured him.

"Just…be careful."

"I always am. That's why I've got half a dozen condoms in my purse."

His jaw dropped open; she laughed.

"Relax, Trav. I'm kidding."

He closed his mouth, cleared his throat. "Actually, I

hope you're not kidding. Not that I want to know about your sex life—or even if you have one—but if you do, you should take precautions."

He was adorably flustered and earnestly sincere, and she lifted herself up on tiptoes to kiss his cheek. "Thanks for the sex ed lesson, big brother. I'll keep that in mind."

Sutter didn't pay too much attention to the speed limit on the way to the ranch, and when he got back to Clayton's house, he took a quick shower. He'd made some progress with Paige today, as evidenced by the fact that she'd been the one to suggest they extend their date to include dinner, and he was determined to build on it.

But he knew that if he left her alone for too long, if he gave her too much time to think, she might change her mind about going out for dinner with him. And he didn't want to risk that happening.

Less than an hour after he'd dropped her off, he was back at her house, freshly showered and cleanly shaven, but there was no response to his knock on the door. Her car was in the driveway and there were lights on inside, so he knocked louder.

Finally the door was flung open. "Sorry," Paige said. "I'm running a little behind schedule."

A fact that was verified by the thick terry robe she was wearing and her dripping-wet hair. He stepped into the foyer.

"My brother stopped by," she explained. "Not for any particular reason as far as I could tell, but…"

He was only half-listening to her words, far more intrigued by the droplet of water that was slowly tracking its way down her throat, then over her collarbone before finally disappearing into the hollow between her breasts.

He didn't have to be a rocket scientist to figure that

she'd heard the knock at the door and thrown on her robe without even toweling herself dry. Which meant that she was naked beneath the robe, and that one tug of the belt knotted at her waist would—

He forced himself to sever the thought and curled his fingers into his palms to resist the urge to reach for her.

"Sutter?"

He yanked his gaze from her chest. "Yeah?"

She huffed out a breath and drew the lapels closer together. Despite her apparent indignation, the flush in her cheeks and the darkening of those chocolate-colored eyes proved that she was feeling the same awareness that was heating his blood.

"I said there's beer and soda in the fridge, if you want a drink while you're waiting."

"Sorry, I wasn't paying attention," he admitted. "I was thinking about how incredibly hot you look right now."

She pushed her sodden bangs away from her face. "I'm a complete mess."

"Do you remember when we cut through the woods on the way home from that party at Brooks Smith's house and you slipped on the log bridge?"

She shuddered at the memory. "It wouldn't have been a big deal if I'd fallen into water, but the recent drought had reduced the stream to a trickle, and I ended up covered in muck and leaves."

And when they'd got back to the ranch, they'd stripped out of their muddy clothes and washed one another under the warm spray of the shower. Of course, the scrubbing away of dirt had soon turned into something else, and they'd made love until the water turned cold.

"Even then—covered in mud from head to toe—you were beautiful."

"You only said that because you wanted to get me naked."

"Just because I wanted to get you naked doesn't mean it wasn't true. And speaking of naked..."

"I should put some clothes on," Paige realized.

"Don't go to any trouble on my account."

She lifted her brows.

He smiled. "Actually, I didn't mean that as a come-on."

"Really?"

He gently brushed the pad of his thumb beneath her eye. "You look tired."

"I thought I was beautiful."

He smiled. "Incredibly beautiful, but tired. And if you don't feel up to going out, I can go to Buffalo Bart's to get some takeout."

He could tell that she was tempted. But she was also wary. No doubt she was thinking about the fact that take-out would mean coming back here, to her house, where they would be alone together. She shook her head.

"I appreciate the offer," she said, already heading for the stairs. "But I think it would be better if we went out."

"Even if I promise not to jump your bones?"

She paused on the bottom step and sent him a sassy smile. "Maybe you should be worried that I might jump yours."

Chapter Seven

When Sutter pulled into the parking lot of the Ace in the Hole, it was mostly full. Of course, dining options in Rust Creek Falls were extremely limited. Aside from this loosely termed bar and grill (which was much more bar than grill and definitely rough around the edges), there was Buffalo Bart's for wings and a few other fast foods, and Daisy's Donut Shop for coffee, pastries and light lunch fare.

Paige recognized several vehicles in the lot, and belatedly accepted that walking through the door beside Sutter could very well escalate what was supposed to be a casual dinner to an event. Most of the longtime residents knew that Paige and Sutter had been an item in high school and beyond, and not one of them would have been surprised to hear the ring of wedding bells for the two of them. But that wasn't how things had played out. Instead, Sutter had spoken out against his brother's decision to reenlist and had left Rust Creek Falls, and Paige had been left nursing her broken heart.

Sutter pulled open the door and gestured for her to enter. As they made their way to a vacant booth, several people lifted their hands in greeting or spoke a few words, and Paige didn't doubt that they were the subjects of some murmured conversations. There had been speculation, of course, after she'd spoken up in Sutter's defense at the mayoral debate, but most of that had died down within a few days because they hadn't been seen out and about together. Being here tonight changed that.

"I should have asked if your sister was working before we came in here," he said, sliding into the seat across from her.

"My sister?"

"Lani," he clarified. "I came in last week for a burger and she was my waitress."

"She doesn't actually work here," Paige told him. "She just fills in for a friend sometimes. Courtney works at a couple of different places and Rosey can't always schedule her hours around the other job, so whenever there's a conflict, she asks Lani to cover her shift."

"That's good, because if Lani was relying on tips to pay her bills, she should learn something about customer service."

Paige grinned ruefully. "I'm sorry if she gave you a hard time."

"You don't have to apologize for your sister," he told her. "And I can't blame her for being mad at me. Because I can see that from her perspective I didn't just leave Rust Creek Falls—I left you."

Paige shrugged, forced herself to respond casually. "From my perspective, too, but I survived."

"I never doubted that you would. And at the time, I didn't see that I had any other choice but to go," he confided. "Although I realize now that leaving town so soon after Forrest reenlisted only cemented everyone's impression that I didn't support him or his military career."

The waitress—and it was Courtney who was working in their section tonight—came to take their drink order. Sutter asked for a draft beer and Paige nodded to indicate that she would have the same. Usually she preferred wine, but the selection at the Ace in the Hole was limited to red or white house wine, which was whatever happened to be the cheapest bottle available from Crawford's that week.

She waited until Courtney had gone to get their drinks before she responded to his comment. "It doesn't matter what other people thought—or even what they think now."

"That sounds good in theory," he agreed. "But the first time I came back to Rust Creek Falls, Clovis Hart wouldn't let me fill up my tank at the gas station."

"You're kidding."

He shook his head. "I knew that speaking out against Forrest's decision wouldn't go over well with a lot of people—but I didn't expect it would make me persona non grata to the whole town.

"By the time I got to the Triple T, I was on empty. I had to ask Braden to come into town with jerry cans so that I would have enough fuel to drive out of town again."

"I'm surprised you ever wanted to come back again after that," she admitted softly.

"Despite the falling out with my family, they're still my family," he told her. "And despite the fact that our relationship was over, I still looked for you every time I was home. I didn't expect a smile or even a wave, I just hoped to catch a glimpse of you in a crowd somewhere."

"I tried to lie low whenever I heard that you were in town," she admitted. "Because it hurt too much to see you."

"It hurt me, too. You were such a huge part of my life, and then…" His words trailed off as Courtney returned with their beverages.

She set the glasses down. "Did you want anything to eat or just the drinks?"

"We definitely want food," Sutter said, looking to Paige for direction.

"We'll share the nachos grande," she decided.

"For an appetizer maybe," Sutter said.

"Bring the nachos," Paige said to Courtney. "We can order something else after that if we're still hungry."

"Nachos," he said, shaking his head after Courtney had gone.

"They've upsized the order since you left. The nachos are more than enough for both of us," Paige assured him.

"I guess we'll find out," he said. "But next time, I'm taking you to Kalispell to a real restaurant."

She sipped her beer. "What makes you think there's going to be a next time?"

"You had a good time today," he reminded her.

"I did," she agreed. "But I'm already having second thoughts about being here with you."

"So I'm not the only one who feels like an animal trapped in an enclosure at the zoo with spectators pressed against the fence staring at us?"

"No, you're not."

"I don't care if people talk about me—I'm used to it," he said sincerely. "But I don't want to make things difficult for you."

She lifted her glass to her lips. "I guess it just bothers me that everyone who sees us together automatically assumes I'm going to fall for you again—and have my heart broken all over again."

"Everyone?"

"My sisters, my brothers, my friends—even Irene Murphy in the feed department at Crawford's warned be to be careful."

"I would never intentionally hurt you," Sutter told her.

"I know," she said, and she did know. But his lack of

intent hadn't prevented it from happening. When he'd left Rust Creek Falls—and left her—she'd felt as if her heart had been ripped out of her chest.

Yes, he'd asked her to go with him, but he had to have known there was no way she could do so when she was in the middle of her required yearlong in-class supervised teaching experience. And he hadn't been willing to wait five months for her to finish. In fact, he'd been so eager to get out of town she doubted he would have been willing to wait five days.

Thankfully, she'd had her teaching to keep her busy. The work—her own and that of her students—occupied most of her waking hours throughout the day. But for the longest time, dreams of Sutter continued to haunt her nights, and she'd wake up in the morning missing him.

He'd been gone about a year, and she was almost halfway through her first year as a "real" teacher when she decided that she'd been missing him long enough. When she'd crossed paths with Jeremy Wellwood, a local high school teacher, at a conference and he'd asked her to go out, she'd accepted the invitation, determined to forget about Sutter once and for all.

They'd gone into Kalispell to the North Bay Grille for dinner. The meal had been delicious and Paige had really enjoyed chatting with Jeremy and getting to know him a little bit better. They'd talked some more on the drive back to Rust Creek Falls, and when he'd walked her to her door and Paige had thanked him for a wonderful evening, she had been sincerely grateful because she'd had an excellent meal and fascinating company and she hadn't thought of Sutter at all…. Okay, maybe she'd thought of him once or twice, but he hadn't preoccupied her every thought, and that was definite progress as far as she was concerned.

Jeremy was an attractive man, and if her heart didn't beat a little bit faster when he smiled at her, that didn't mean she wasn't attracted to him. She'd figured that only proved that she wasn't a schoolgirl anymore. She was simply past the stage where she was going to get all starry-eyed and weak-kneed over anyone.

And then Jeremy had kissed her. His lips were a little too soft, a little too moist and his technique a little too practiced. Or maybe it was just that his lips weren't Sutter's lips. And when he'd touched her, she'd wanted to pull away rather than lean into him. Because his hands weren't Sutter's hands.

Alone in her bed that night, she'd realized that she'd been subconsciously comparing every man she met to Sutter—and had found them all lacking in some way. The realization frustrated her, because she wanted to share her life with someone, to marry and have a family. For years she'd believed she would have that family with Sutter. But he'd made it clear that he had no intention of coming back to Rust Creek Falls for anything more than the occasional visit, so she had to stop wanting what she couldn't have and think realistically about her future.

When Jeremy called her again, she'd ignored her reservations and agreed to another date. Over the next few months, there were several more dates until she finally decided she was ready to take the final step. The next time he'd invited her back to his place, she'd accepted. She had sex with him, and after she went home, she'd cried herself to sleep.

He called her the day after, but she admitted that she was still not completely over her ex. It didn't seem to matter that Sutter had been gone for almost two years. He was still firmly entrenched in her heart.

She felt horrible about what had happened with Jeremy. She'd liked him and enjoyed spending time with him, but she hadn't cared about him as much as she'd cared about proving that her relationship with Sutter was firmly in the past. She'd thought that sleeping with someone else would make her forget the only man she'd ever loved. Instead, it had proved to her that physical intimacy without real emotion was cheap and meaningless.

After that, she'd vowed that she wouldn't fall into bed with another man until she was sure that she genuinely cared about him and could imagine a future for them together. Alex Monroe was supposed to have been that man, and she'd honestly thought they were heading in that direction—until Sutter came back to town.

She was twenty-seven years old and she'd had only two lovers. She wasn't sure if that was admirable or pathetic. Was her limited experience a reflection of discriminatory taste or simple disinterest? And what did it mean that her formerly dormant libido was humming whenever she was around Sutter?

Thankfully, Courtney returned to their table, saving Paige from further introspection.

The nachos were heaped on a platter and layered with spicy ground beef, melted cheeses, diced tomatoes, sliced black olives and jalapeños, with bowls of sour cream and salsa on the side. Sutter's eyes widened when the waitress slid the platter into the middle of the table.

"Still think you're going to need more than this?" Paige teased him.

He shrugged. "I guess that depends on how much you're going to eat."

She lifted a chip heavy with meat and cheese from the top of the platter. "As much as I can."

He grinned and gestured for Courtney to bring them a couple more drinks.

They both dug into the chips, eating more than talk-ing until they'd devoured half of them. The nachos were salty and spicy, and Paige downed her second draft fairly quickly. She'd never been a heavy drinker, but she was thirsty and the beer went down easily, so when Courtney asked if she wanted another, she nodded. Sutter shook his head in response to the same question but ordered a soda, no doubt conscious of the fact that he was driving.

"I almost forgot how much you liked Mexican," he noted.

Paige wasn't eating with as much enthusiasm now, but she continued to pick at the chips. "My second favorite kind of food."

"What's the first?"

"Anything sweet," she admitted.

"I'd love to take you to Seattle sometime," he said. "There's a little restaurant tucked at the end of a residen-tial street that serves seriously authentic Mexican. The menu is written in Spanish, the tamales are homemade and the margaritas are icy and tart."

Her brows lifted. "You don't strike me as the mar-garita type."

"I'm not," he admitted. "But Jenni guzzles them down like water."

She didn't want to ask. His life in Seattle was none of her business, but he'd dropped the name so easily, her curiosity was undeniably piqued. "Who's Jenni?"

"Jenni Locke—the head trainer at my stable."

"I thought most trainers were men."

"I'd say the majority probably are," he agreed. "But there are increasing numbers of women in the field and I have to say Jenni is one of the best I've ever known."

She traced the ring of condensation on the table with her fingertip. "How long has she been with you?"

"Since the beginning."

"You must know her pretty well, then."

"You work closely with someone for three years, you get to know them pretty well," he agreed.

"Are you…involved?"

He paused with a nacho halfway to his mouth. "What?"

She shook her head. She hadn't meant to ask the question and wasn't sure she wanted to know the answer. "Forget it."

Of course he didn't forget it. Instead, he said, "Do you mean *romantically* involved?"

"I shouldn't have asked. It's none of my business."

He dropped the nacho onto his plate. "I would have thought you knew me better than to think I'd be kissing you if I was involved with someone else."

"Five years is a long time," she reminded him. "I'm not sure I know you at all anymore."

"I haven't changed, not that much. And to answer your question—no. Jenni and I are not, and never have been, romantically involved.

"She is, however, one of my best friends in Seattle. In fact, she and Reese, my stable manager, are probably my two best friends. Although that might be simply because we spend so much time together," he admitted wryly. "But we also have a lot in common, including a vested interest in the success of Traub Stables."

She hesitated on the verge of asking another question to which she might not like the answer, but decided that she had to know. "Do you miss being there?"

"I miss the routines," he admitted. "I miss looking around and knowing that everything I see is mine." He held her gaze across the table. "But right now, I don't want to be anywhere but exactly where I am."

And right now, that was enough for Paige.

* * *

Paige nibbled on a few more chips, then pushed the platter closer to Sutter. "I'm done."

He was close to being done himself but unwilling to admit defeat. He picked up a nacho and dunked it in salsa.

"How about you?" he asked her. "Do you love teaching as much as you thought you would?"

"Even more," she said, then stifled a yawn.

"Tired?"

She nodded. "It's been a long day."

"And a busy one," he agreed.

"But it's starting to look like we might actually make our target of having the school ready for the new year."

"Which means you'll get your living room back."

She smiled. "I don't mind so much. It beats the alternative of not being able to hold classes at all—I can't imagine the kind of mischief some of my students would get into if there wasn't any structure to their days."

"That would be their parents' problem, not yours," he pointed out.

"Says the man from the big city."

"What's that supposed to mean?"

"Just that maybe you have forgotten how things work in towns like this—any problem is everyone's problem, whether it's a natural disaster or a kid who goes around causing trouble because he's got too much time on his hands."

"What about a kid who swipes a red licorice rope in a misguided attempt to impress a pretty girl?"

"Usually a parent's reprimand is sufficient to ensure that kind of delinquent behavior doesn't become a habit."

"I was reprimanded by my father's hand on my butt," he reminded her.

"And I kissed your cheek to apologize for getting you into trouble."

"Not the one that hurt."

She smiled. "I'd almost forgotten about that."

"I didn't," he told her. "I was ten years old, and it was my first kiss."

"And I still have a weakness for red rope licorice," she admitted.

"I'll keep that in mind." He leaned back in his seat and picked up his soda. Looking around, he noticed the empty stage at the back of the room. "Do they ever have live music here anymore?"

"Maybe two or three times a year. Rosey figures the jukebox is all she needs to provide in the way of musical entertainment—and it's already paid for."

"Then she hasn't changed at all in the past five years," he mused.

"The only thing that's changed is the menu," Paige told him. "Although wings and burgers are probably still the most popular items, she did upgrade the nachos and added wraps and even salads."

"Salads?"

"Not standard cowboy fare," she acknowledged. "But it has brought more women here at lunchtime."

The jukebox Paige mentioned had been eating up quarters all night with a standard assortment of country-and-western tunes playing consistently in the background, so he was pleasantly surprised to hear one of Shania Twain's biggest hits start up.

"Do you remember this song?" Sutter asked.

Paige nodded but kept her gaze firmly fixed on the glass she held between her hands. "It was a huge hit when we were in high school."

"*And* the first song we danced to at your junior prom," he reminded her.

She just nodded again.

He glanced toward the center of the room, where a few couples had ventured onto the dance floor. He tipped his head in that direction. "What do you think—want to hit the dance floor for old times' sake?"

This time, she shook her head. "No, thanks."

"Why not?"

"People started talking as soon as we walked through the front door—imagine how the goship would spread if we stepped onto the dance floor together."

"I'm not afraid of a little gossip."

"'Cuz you don't live here."

"Was it really that bad when I left?"

"No," she said. "It was worse. And not jus' 'cuz people talked about our breakup, but 'cuz they all felt sorry for me. 'Poor Paige—dumped and abandoned by her boyfriend.'"

He winced. "You should have told them the truth—that *you* dumped *me.*"

"I didn't *dump* you. I wanted you to stay." She picked up her glass again and frowned when she discovered that it was empty.

"Did you want anything else? Soda? Coffee?" He didn't suggest another beer because he'd noticed, even if she hadn't, that she was starting to slur her words just a little.

"No," she decided, shaking her head. "I'm ready to go."

He paid the bill, then stood up. She slid out of the booth, ignoring the hand he offered to her. He figured it was like the dance floor—she didn't want to give the locals anything to talk about.

The rusty hinges of the screen door protested when she pushed it open. She paused on the porch to draw in a deep breath of the cold night air.

Sutter stopped beside her. "Are you okay?"

"I'm not sure," she admitted. "My ears are buzzing, and my head's floating—" she held a hand about six inches over her head "—somewhere around here."

"You never were much of a drinker," he remembered.

"I'm still not." She drew in another breath. "I prob'ly shouldn't have had the shecond beer."

"I think it's more likely the third that you're feeling."

She turned her head to look at him, her brow furrowed. "I didn't have three."

"Yeah, you did."

"Well, that would 'splain the buzzing in my ears."

He led her to his truck, helped her into the cab and made sure she was buckled in before he went around to the driver's side.

She didn't say much on the short drive back to her house. When he pulled into her driveway, he realized it was because she'd fallen asleep. He opened her door and nudged her awake.

"Come on, sleeping beauty. You're home."

He walked her to the door to make sure she got inside safely. He didn't intend to go any farther, except that she squinted at the key she pulled out of her pocket and couldn't quite slide it into the lock. He covered her hand with his own to help guide her movements. The deadbolt released, and he turned the knob.

"Do you have any acetaminophen?"

"D'you have a headache?"

He smiled. "Not for me—for you."

"I don't have a headache," she told him.

"You might in the morning," he warned.

She went to the kitchen, poured herself a glass of water and shook a couple of tablets out of the bottle she located in the cupboard.

"You want me to take you up to your bed now?"

She looked up at him, her solemn gaze considering him. "Yeah," she admitted on a sigh. "But I don' think thatsa good idea."

Chapter Eight

Sutter had to smile, not just at her erroneous interpretation of the question but her unexpected reply to it.

"I was only asking if you wanted me to help you upstairs and get you settled," he clarified, though his own thoughts had now shifted in a very different direction.

"You can't help me get shettled—you make me *un*-shettled."

"Not nearly as unsettled as you make me, I'll bet."

"D'you ever lie awake at night thinkin' 'bout me and wishin' I was there?"

"Every night," he admitted.

"D'you dream 'bout me?"

"Every night," he said again.

"Good," she decided. "'Cuz I dream 'bout you, too."

"What do you dream about?" he asked, because he was curious and she seemed to be in the mood to talk.

Her lips curved as her eyes drifted shut. "I dream 'bout you kissing me, touching me. And it's so real.... I can almost feel your hands on my body." She took his hands now and moved them to her breasts. "I *want* to feel your hands on my body."

Oh, damn—he had *not* anticipated this, and his own body's response was immediate and undeniable. As all the blood in his head migrated south, he knew he should pull his hands away, but hers held his immobile, and he felt her nipples bead beneath his palms.

"Touch me," she said.

He couldn't seem to help himself. His fingers gently kneaded the tender flesh; his thumbs brushed over the tight buds. She moaned low in her throat, a sensual sound of appreciation that made his whole body ache with want.

"Kiss me."

There was no way he could refuse. Not that she gave him much choice in the matter. Even before the words were out of her mouth, her hands were linked behind his head, urging his mouth down to hers.

She might be feeling some effects from the alcohol, but it hadn't affected her coordination at all. She fastened her mouth on his in a kiss that was soft and warm and incredibly sweet. Then her tongue slid between his lips to dance with his, and the flavor changed to something hotter, spicier and infinitely more dangerous.

In some distant part of his brain, it occurred to Sutter that one of them should think about this rationally—and he didn't think it was going to be Paige. With sincere re-luctance, he eased his mouth from hers.

"It's late," he said.

Her only response was to take his hand and start up the stairs.

Since Sutter was pretty sure she was heading toward her bedroom, he tried to hold back. "I really have to be going."

But his resistance made her stumble on the next step. With a muttered oath, he scooped her into his arms and carried her up.

"First room on the right," she told him.

He stepped just inside the door and set her back on her feet. She slipped her hands beneath the hem of his T-shirt, slid her palms over his chest. She pushed the fabric up and pressed her lips to his chest, where his heart was beating a frantic and desperate rhythm.

He tugged her hands away. "Honey, you're just a little bit—" *Topless,* he realized, his jaw on the floor. Before he'd managed to get a complete sentence out of his mouth, she'd tossed her shirt aside and her bra had immediately followed.

She'd asked him to touch her, to kiss her, and he wanted to do that and a whole lot more. But he was a grown man with at least a tiny bit of self-control, and he managed to restrain himself. At least until she took his hands and brought them to her breasts again. His eyes closed, but he didn't know if he should swear or pray for forgiveness, because when she drew him back to the bed, he let her. Then he lowered his head.

He laved her nipple with his tongue, tasting, teasing, then drew the turgid peak into his mouth and suckled. She gasped and arched against him, her fingers threaded through his hair, cupping the back of his head, silently urging him on. He complied, using his lips and tongue and teeth until she was panting and squirming.

He wanted to make love with her more than he wanted to take another breath, but it wasn't going to happen tonight. Not when he knew that Paige didn't really know what she was doing. He might curse his conscience, but he couldn't ignore it.

He pulled away and tried to catch his breath and cool his blood. Her pajamas were neatly folded on top of her pillow. He picked up the top and tugged it over her head.

She blinked at him, apparently confused as to why he was suddenly dressing her instead of *un*dressing her. As he tugged the long-sleeved shirt into place, he kissed her again, because he was afraid that if he gave her a chance to say anything else, he might forget all the reasons that making love with her tonight was a bad idea.

Her hand slid between their bodies to rub over the front of his jeans, where his erection was straining painfully. "You do want me," she realized.

"Wanting isn't the problem."

"Wha's the problem?"

"Three beers," he muttered, and moved off of the bed. She blinked. "Huh?"

"When we make love, I want to be sure you'll remember it in the morning."

"I'll remember," she told him. "I've never been able to forget."

He picked up her pajama bottoms, holding them out at arm's length to her.

"No one else has ever made me forget," she said as she snatched them out of his hand.

"Forget what?"

She stood up abruptly—and swayed just a little when she got to her feet. He started to reach out to steady her, then dropped his hand again, deciding that any physical contact at this point could be more dangerous than Paige falling over.

She unsnapped the button at the front of her jeans and began wiggling out of the snug-fitting denim. He knew he should look away—if not for the sake of her modesty then for his own peace of mind. But the slow, sensual movement of her hips held him spellbound.

"How it felt to make love with you," she finally answered his question.

When the denim pooled at her feet, she was clad in a pair of pale pink bikini panties with delicate lace trim. He swallowed hard and took a deliberate step back, away from her.

"You're not the only man I've ever been with." She finally covered up those delectable little panties with her pajama bottoms. Also pink but decorated with fat white cartoon sheep.

"I didn't expect that I was," he said. He hoped she wouldn't name names, because he was wound up tight enough right now to want to hunt down all of her other lovers and beat them mercilessly for daring to touch the only woman he'd ever loved.

She pulled back the covers on her bed. "I thought if I slept with shomeone else, I'd fin'ly get over you."

He'd fallen into the same trap too many times before he'd accepted the truth: he would never get over Paige. He could build a new life and even have other relationships, but she would always own his heart.

He moved forward now, but only to pull the comforter up over her. "If it's all the same to you, I'd really rather not hear about your other lovers right now."

"Lover," she said, rubbing her cheek against her pillow.

He stilled. "What?"

"Singular, not plural." She yawned. "There was only one after you."

He stood there for a minute, trying to make sense of what she was saying. The words were simple enough, but the implications were enormous. And his heart seemed to swell inside his chest, buoyed by the possibility that she might still love him, too.

"I bet you've been with lotsa women," she murmured.

Now that she was snuggled under the blankets, he figured it was safe enough to sit on the edge of the mattress. He gently brushed her hair off of her cheek. "No one who ever made me forget about you," he told her honestly.

"You shouldn'ta come back."

"Do you really wish I'd stayed away?"

"No," she admitted. "I wish you'd never gone."

"Since I'm here now, will you spend the day with me tomorrow?"

Her eyes were starting to close. "Thas not a good idea."

"Let's try a different answer," he suggested, and brushed his lips gently over hers. "Say, 'Yes, I'll spend the day with you, Sutter.'"

"Yes, I'll spend the day…" The words trailed off as she drifted into sleep.

Paige awoke in the morning with her throat dry and her head pounding. She eased herself carefully up in bed and pressed her hands to her throbbing temples. A quick glance at the clock revealed that it was almost ten o'clock. Beside the clock was a glass of water, a bottle of acetaminophen and a note: "Take two, drink all the water and call me when you're up." Sutter hadn't signed it, but he had left his cell phone number.

She took the two pills, drank the water and headed to the shower.

There were some fuzzy patches in her memory of the previous evening. Not of the time they were at the Ace in the Hole, but afterward. She thought she'd dozed off on the drive home, then she remembered Sutter walking her to the door.

Had he kissed her good-night?

Her mind suddenly flashed with an image of his hard, strong body pressed against hers. Of those strong, talented hands stroking her skin. Of his hot, hungry mouth devouring hers. Was it a memory or just a fantasy? Either way, the mental picture had her blood racing and her heart pounding, so maybe it was better that she didn't remember.

And it would be really good if she could clear all thoughts of Sutter from her mind before she walked into church.

Her family was already seated in their usual row when she arrived, but she hovered at the back for a few minutes, waiting until the service was about to begin before taking her place beside Lindsay. She figured her tardiness would save her from any interrogation. In truth, it only delayed it.

When the service was over and everyone filed out again, her parents went downstairs for their usual coffee and chitchat with friends and neighbors. Sometimes Paige and her sisters would join them, but she declined the invitation today and Lani and Lindsay opted to leave with her.

"I didn't see Alex in church," Lani noted.

"That's not unusual," Paige said.

"I know," her sister admitted. "But Mom was hoping to invite him to dinner tonight."

"That would be a little awkward," Paige warned.

"Why?"

"Because we broke up."

"When?" Lani demanded.

"A few days ago."

"Are you seeing Sutter now?" Lindsay asked.

"No," she replied, immediately and firmly.

"But you were at the school with him yesterday," Lani noted.

"Yes, because Sutter was bugging me to go out with him, and I suggested that we go to the school as an alternative."

"And after you finished at the school?" Lindsay prompted.

Paige sighed. "Obviously you know someone who saw us at the bar last night."

"Half the town saw you at the Ace in the Hole last night," Lani informed her.

"We were at the school late, and we were both hungry when we finished, so we went to grab a bite to eat."

"Did he kiss you good-night?" Lindsay asked.

"I'm not getting involved with Sutter," Paige said firmly.

Her sisters exchanged glances.

"He kissed her good-night," Lani decided, not sounding the least bit happy about it.

She sighed. "Yes, he kissed me. But that's no reason to make it into something bigger than it is."

"I still can't believe you dumped Alex," Lani grumbled. "He's a great guy."

"He is a great guy," Paige agreed. "And I didn't dump him."

Her sister rolled her eyes. "I doubt he dumped you."

"It was a mutual decision," Paige told them.

"So he wasn't heartbroken?" Lani challenged.

"He definitely wasn't heartbroken," she confirmed.

"Did you want him to be?"

"Of course not," Paige denied. "But considering that we've been dating for a few months, I didn't expect him to be so...unaffected."

"Which, I guess, tells you everything you needed to know about that relationship," Lindsay noted.

"I did really like Alex."

"But he's not Sutter."

"Will you stop trying to make this about Sutter?"

Lani shook her head. "Will you stop trying to pretend this is about anything but Sutter? If he hadn't come back to Rust Creek Falls, if he hadn't kissed you and made you remember what the two of you used to have together, you'd still be with Alex."

"We're just worried about you, Paige," Lindsay said gently.

Paige understood that her sisters were thinking about what was best for her—and no doubt remembering how completely heartbroken she'd been when Sutter had left Rust Creek Falls five years earlier. "I appreciate that," she told them. "But I assure you, there's no reason to worry. I'm not going to get hung up on Sutter again.

"Yes, I've kissed the guy a couple of times. And yes, he is a fabulous kisser. But I have no illusions that a few kisses are going to lead to anything else, because I know that Sutter isn't going to stay in Rust Creek Falls."

"And if he asks you to go to Seattle with him again?"

She just shook her head. "He's never even hinted in that direction, and he knows that my life is here."

"I know that's what you said five years ago," Lindsay agreed. "Because you were trying to convince Sutter to stay, and because you didn't want to be too far away when Gram was so sick. But even when he packed up and left town, you waited for him to come back. You didn't believe he would stay in Seattle for five months—never mind five years."

She was right. Paige hadn't expected that Sutter's move would be permanent. She hadn't believed he would stay away from his family. She hadn't wanted to believe that he would stay away from her. But when she'd refused to go with him, he'd taken that to mean that their relationship was over. She'd tried to explain all the reasons that the timing wasn't good, but he was determined to go—with or without her.

And still she'd thought he would return. But the days had turned into weeks, the weeks into months and the heart that had felt so battered and bruised by his decision to leave Rust Creek Falls had shattered into a billion pieces.

She'd thought about going after him—more times than she wanted to admit. She'd thought about packing up and following him to wherever he was. Because her life felt so empty without him, because she felt incomplete without him.

But even after her grandmother had finally lost her battle with multiple sclerosis and passed away, Paige had had her pride. It hadn't kept her warm at night, but it had refused to let her chase after him. Besides, she'd believed that what she'd told him was true. He had to make peace with his family, and he was never going to do that from five hundred miles away.

And truthfully, she'd been more than a little insecure about their relationship at that point, and terrified by the thought of leaving everything familiar to start a new life in unfamiliar surroundings. It was a testament to how much she'd loved Sutter that she'd even considered it, but his willingness to leave his family in the face of conflict made her wonder if some kind of disagreement might cause him to leave her, too. In the end, that was exactly what happened—they'd had differing opinions as to how he should handle the clash with his family, and he'd left.

The fact that he'd come home now, that he'd heard about the flood and had come back to help his family, gave her hope that he hadn't turned his back on Rust Creek Falls completely. But if he thought his return meant that he could just pick back up where he'd left off with

Paige, he was sorely mistaken. She wasn't going to give him another chance to break her heart.

The problem was, she enjoyed spending time with Sutter. She felt comfortable with him—maybe too comfortable. Because she inevitably let her guard down around him, which meant that she would have to make a concerted effort to avoid him. A more difficult task than she'd imagined when she turned onto her street and saw his vehicle parked in front of her house.

The shiny new truck with the Washington State plates stood out from the more weathered pickups that most of the locals drove and was a tangible reminder of how far he'd gone since he'd left Rust Creek Falls—and proof that he'd chosen to make his life somewhere else and without her.

With that thought in mind, she steeled her resolve and met him on the porch. "What are you doing here, Sutter?"

"I'm here to pick you up."

"Why?"

"Because you got to choose what we did yesterday, so today it's my turn."

"Except that I never agreed to do anything with you today."

"Actually you did," he told her.

She frowned. "When?"

"Last night. When I brought you home after dinner."

Since her memories of last night were still a little fuzzy, she couldn't say for certain that she hadn't. "You had to know that I had a little too much to drink last night."

"How is the head today?"

"Fine." *Now.* "But I'm a little bit…hazy on what was said after we left the restaurant, which means I can't be held responsible for any agreements I might have made. And if you were an honorable man—"

"If I *wasn't* an honorable man, we would have had this conversation several hours ago—in your bed."

That snagged her attention. "What are you talking about?"

"You invited me to spend the night with you."

Her cheeks flamed as the fantasy/memory of their bodies pressed close together shimmered in her mind again.

"I did not," she said, but her denial lacked both strength and conviction.

"You did, too," he told her. "Lucky for you, I realized that you weren't thinking clearly and I didn't take you up on the offer. But I was more than a little tempted."

"I wouldn't have let anything go that far—I don't sleep around."

"I know."

The simple, matter-of-fact statement made her wonder. "Did I tell you that last night, too?"

"Yep," he agreed.

Three beers and she apparently lost not only her inhibitions but control of her mouth. "Did I admit that I've only slept with half a dozen other guys since you left?"

"Actually you said it was only one."

His words made her humiliation complete. Not only had she been intoxicated enough to throw herself at him, but her lack of a sex life since he'd been gone was tantamount to an admission that she'd never gotten over him.

A change of topic was definitely in order. "My parents are expecting me at their house by five o'clock for dinner."

"I'll make sure you're back before five," he promised. "So what did you want to do today?"

* * *

He took her to the Triple T.

Paige should have suspected they would be going to the ranch when Sutter suggested that she change her clothes. She swapped the long skirt she'd worn to church for a pair of jeans and tugged a thick sweater on over her blouse, then tucked her feet into a pair of cowboy boots.

When she realized where they were headed, the nerves inside her belly started to twist into knots. She had more than a few reservations about their destination, mostly because there were so many memories for her at his family's ranch and she didn't want those memories dredged up. Or maybe she was more worried about the feelings evoked by those memories.

He drove past the family homestead and parked his truck by the barn. There were a couple of horses saddled and tethered in the closest paddock. "Obviously Rusty got my message," he said, guiding her toward the waiting animals.

Just the sight of the gorgeous palomino with the golden coat and luxurious blond mane and tail made Paige's throat tighten. Buttercup was the mount that she'd always used when she'd gone riding with Sutter at the Triple T, and she'd sincerely missed the horse when she'd stopped going out to the ranch after he'd gone.

"Do you remember Buttercup?"

"Of course," she admitted, stroking the animal's muzzle with easy affection. "But I don't recognize her companion. Where's Maverick?"

"I took him to Seattle with me."

"Oh. Of course." She should have realized that. Maverick had been Sutter's pride and joy. He'd raised him and trained him, and it made perfect sense that he would have taken the horse with him when he left.

YOUR PARTICIPATION IS REQUESTED!

Dear Reader,

Since you are a lover of romance fiction – we would like to get to know you!

Inside you will find a short Reader's Survey. Sharing your answers with us will help our editorial staff understand who you are and what activities you enjoy.

To thank you for your participation, we would like to send you 2 books and 2 gifts – **ABSOLUTELY FREE!**

Enjoy your gifts with our appreciation,

Pam Powers

SEE INSIDE FOR READER'S SURVEY

For Your Romance Reading Pleasure...

FREE!

We'll send you 2 books and 2 gifts
ABSOLUTELY FREE
just for completing our Reader's Survey!

YOUR READER'S SURVEY
"THANK YOU" FREE GIFTS INCLUDE:
► 2 Harlequin® Special Edition books
► 2 lovely surprise gifts

PLEASE FILL IN THE CIRCLES COMPLETELY TO RESPOND

1) What type of fiction books do you enjoy reading? (Check all that apply)
   ○ Suspense/Thrillers   ○ Action/Adventure   ○ Modern-day Romances
   ○ Historical Romance   ○ Humour   ○ Paranormal Romance

2) What attracted you most to the last fiction book you purchased on impulse?
   ○ The Title   ○ The Cover   ○ The Author   ○ The Story

3) What is usually the greatest influencer when you <u>plan</u> to buy a book?
   ○ Advertising   ○ Referral   ○ Book Review

4) How often do you access the internet?
   ○ Daily ○ Weekly ○ Monthly ○ Rarely or never.

5) How many NEW paperback fiction novels have you purchased in the past 3 months?
   ○ 0 - 2   ○ 3 - 6   ○ 7 or more

YES! I have completed the Reader's Survey. Please send me the 2 FREE books and 2 FREE gifts (gifts are worth about $10) for which I qualify. I understand that I am under no obligation to purchase any books, as explained on the back of this card.

235/335 HDL F5C5

FIRST NAME	LAST NAME

ADDRESS

APT.#	CITY

STATE/PROV.	ZIP/POSTAL CODE

"I wanted to take Buttercup, too," he told her now. "Because the two of them were accustomed to spending a lot of time together, but I couldn't do it. It seemed like I'd be taking her away from you."

"So who's this?" she asked, nodding her head toward the bay gelding with the white blaze on his forehead.

"Toby," he said, and the horse whinnied in acknowledgment.

"Smart," she noted.

The horse nodded his big head; Paige chuckled.

"I packed a picnic lunch for us," Sutter said, checking the saddlebags to ensure it was there. "I figured we'd both be hungry after being out in the fresh air for a while."

"How long is a while?"

"I promised to have you home before five o'clock, and I will," Sutter assured.

"I wasn't thinking about the time so much as I was thinking about my butt," she admitted. "I haven't been on the back of a horse in a long time."

The statement seemed to surprise him. "You used to love riding."

"I loved riding with you." And when he was gone, it wasn't the same. Besides, it wasn't as if she could just take a drive out to the Triple T and saddle up one of the horses to navigate a familiar trail. Her brothers had horses, but again, it had never been the riding she'd enjoyed as much as the company when she'd been with Sutter.

"Do you want to do this?"

"Right now I do," she said. "But I'm well aware that some long-neglected muscles might regret that decision tomorrow."

"I'm more than willing to give you a full-body massage to help loosen up anything that feels tight when we're done."

"That's an interesting offer—" and more tempting than she was willing to admit, especially when being close to him had her feeling tight and achy all over "—but I think I'll pass."

"Well, if you change your mind…"

"I'll let you know," she promised him.

Chapter Nine

It might have been a while since Paige had been on the back of a horse, but she obviously hadn't forgotten anything. She looked good in the saddle, with the wind blowing her long dark hair away from her face, her cheeks pink with cold and her eyes sparkling with happiness.

They rode for almost an hour before they reached the top of the bluff where they'd spent a lot of time during those long-ago summers. There was a trio of silver maples clustered together on one side of a man-made swimming hole and, low on the trunk of the fattest tree, Sutter had carved a crude heart with "ST + PD" inside it. Paige had added the inscription "4EVR."

"Do you want to walk for a bit, to make sure you can still feel your legs?"

"Sure," Paige agreed.

Sutter dismounted, then took Buttercup's reins to hold her steady so Paige could do the same. She slid to the ground, keeping a hand on the horse's flank to maintain her balance.

"You okay?"

She nodded. "But I think having my feet on the ground for a little bit is a good idea."

They walked in companionable silence for a few minutes, enjoying the quiet of the day and the spectacular scenery of the ranch. He'd grown up on this ranch and had taken it for granted for a lot of years. It was only when he'd moved to Washington that he'd realized how much the Montana landscape was part of his heart and soul. There were a lot of things to love about Seattle, and he did, but it wasn't in his blood the way Rust Creek Falls had always been.

The distinctive "kee-eee-arr" of a red-tailed hawk sounded, and Paige stopped to watch the raptor slowly turning in circles as it surveyed the open field for any sign of prey. "They're such graceful creatures."

"Graceful…and vicious," Sutter noted as the hawk swooped down to snag some unsuspecting critter in its claws.

She winced. "Yeah, that, too."

"I guess that means it must be lunchtime."

"Suddenly I'm not very hungry."

Hungry or not, he saw that she was shivering. "You're cold," he said, and silently cursed himself for not realizing it sooner.

"A little," she admitted. "I didn't realize how chilly it was today."

"You're more sheltered from the wind in town," he noted. "Out here, there are no barriers against Mother Nature or her whims."

"I wouldn't want any," Paige said honestly. "Although I wouldn't have minded a heavier jacket."

"I'd planned for us to have a picnic, but now I'm thinking that's not such a great idea."

"Outdoor picnics are better suited for the summer," she suggested.

"We had a lot of them." He stepped up behind her, partly to block the wind but mostly because it gave him an excuse to be close to her, and wrapped his arms around her. She leaned into his embrace, her head tipped back against his shoulder. "We'd spread a blanket in the sun by the swimming hole, eat whatever we'd managed to steal from my mom's kitchen for lunch, take a dip in the water to cool off if it was hot and sometimes you'd let me kiss you."

He wondered if she ever thought about those long-ago summer days, when they'd spent so much time out here, swimming and kissing and sometimes a whole lot more.

Not that there was any chance of anything like that happening today. It was too cold to even unzip a coat, never mind get naked and busy. Although just thinking about the busy part had him feeling all kinds of hot and bothered on the inside. He banished the enticing thoughts from his mind. "Can you ride a little bit farther?"

"Farther into the middle of nowhere?" she asked warily.

He grinned. "We're not as far away from civilization as you think."

He helped her up into the saddle and then he mounted Toby and started away. Ten minutes later, they'd arrived at their destination.

"This is Clayton's place, isn't it?" Paige asked.

"And my temporary home away from home." Sutter tied up the horses and proceeded to fill the trough so they could drink.

While he was doing that, she unpacked the saddlebags. "You're not staying at the main house?"

"I haven't spent a night under that roof since I left," he admitted.

"Oh, Sutter." Her eyes filled with tears.

"Don't feel sorry for me, Paige. I know why things are the way they are."

"Then maybe you can explain it to me."

"I didn't toe the family line."

"You stated a differing opinion—and you had valid reasons for it."

"Valid doesn't mean forgivable," he told her.

"You have to know your mother didn't mean it when she said that if you couldn't support your brother, you weren't welcome in her home."

"My mother doesn't usually say things she doesn't mean."

She frowned. "Are you telling me that, in the past five years, you've never once talked to her about this?"

He opened the door, gestured for her to enter. "What's to talk about?"

She shook her head. "You need to talk to her," she insisted. "Otherwise you're never going to let go of the hurt you're carrying inside."

He led her through the foyer, past the den on one side and the living room on the other and into the eat-in kitchen at the back. "Coffee?"

"Yes, please."

He measured out the grounds, poured water in the reservoir.

"I was mad at her for a long time, too," Paige commented.

"I'm not mad at her."

"You should be," she said. "You had a disagreement with Forrest and she supported your brother, not just taking the side of one son over the other but doing so publicly."

"Okay, maybe I'm a little mad." He took a couple plates out of the cupboard and unwrapped the sandwiches.

"And hurt."

He opened a bag of potato chips and dumped some onto each of the plates. "Let's eat."

She huffed out an exaggerated breath. "You're such a man."

"Thanks for noticing."

"It won't kill you to talk about your feelings," she told him, carrying the plates to the table.

He poured the coffee into two mugs and took a seat across from her. "And what if you're wrong about that?"

"Okay. I'll tell you about mine," Paige decided.

He picked up half of his sandwich, bit into it.

"I was mad at your mother for a long time, too, because I blamed her for your decision to leave Rust Creek Falls," she confided.

"It wasn't her fault."

"That doesn't matter—feelings don't need to be rational, they just need to be." She looked at the sandwich on her plate: thickly sliced ham between slices of fresh bread slathered with mustard, just the way she liked it. But she picked up her mug, sipped her coffee instead. "And it was easier to blame her than to accept that it might have been my fault."

"It wasn't your fault, either," he said in the same deliberately casual tone.

She nibbled on a chip. "I felt as if I'd let you down— but you let me down, too."

"What did I do?"

"You left."

"I'm pretty sure we talked about that," he said drily.

"But I didn't believe you would actually go," she admitted. "I knew you were angry and upset, but I still didn't think you would leave. And when you did, I was sure you wouldn't be gone for very long." She gave him a wry smile. "Obviously I forgot how stubborn you can be."

"Said the pot to the kettle," he noted wryly.

She opened her mouth to protest, then shut it again. "Okay—I could have called and tried to keep in touch."

He didn't ask why she hadn't, for which she was grateful, because she wasn't entirely sure how she would have answered that question. Because the truth—that it hurt too much to know that he was so far away—was too revealing.

"Speaking of keeping in touch—how are things in Seattle?" she asked in a somewhat desperate attempt to redirect her thoughts. Thinking about her history with Sutter was only going to lead to heartbreak; she needed to remember that his present was far away from Rust Creek Falls—and her.

"Everything seems to be under control."

"Seems to be?"

"I have complete faith in Jenni and Reese."

Jenni, she remembered, was his trainer—the one who drank margaritas. And Reese—she tried to remember what he'd told her about him. "Reese is your stable manager?"

He nodded. "And all-around go-to guy."

"Still, you must be itching to get back and check on things for yourself." She kept her voice light, determined not to let him know how much the knowledge that he would be leaving again tore her up inside. Because he'd made her no promises, and he'd certainly never pretended that he was back in Rust Creek Falls to stay.

"There doesn't seem to be any urgent need, and right now I'm more concerned about what's happening here."

"Everything is on track here—thanks to Lissa Roarke. It's amazing how much attention she's drawn to Rust Creek Falls and the devastation done by the floods."

"I wasn't talking about the status of the town, but the status of us."

"I want us to be friends, Sutter. But anything more than that—" she shook her head "—just isn't going to happen."

Sutter seemed to consider her statement for a long minute before he responded. "I can accept being friends," he finally agreed. Then he flashed the smile that never failed to make her knees weak. "For a start."

As the weather continued to grow colder and the occasional dustings of snow started to accumulate, Paige began to appreciate not having to leave her house to go to work. Although holding classes in her home provided a whole other set of challenges, especially when the kids started bouncing off the walls in anticipation of the upcoming holidays. Right after Halloween, their thoughts had fast-forwarded to Christmas, and every one of her students was excited. Everyone except Ryder.

Paige couldn't help but notice that the more the other kids talked about the upcoming holiday, the more withdrawn Sutter's eldest nephew became. She wished there was some way to reach him—to bring him out of himself and get him involved in something.

A recent staff meeting at the principal's house had included a discussion about the elementary school's annual Christmas production. Some of the teachers wanted to cancel it this year, suggesting that their time and attention were better spent on other things. Paige was relieved when the principal insisted that was exactly why the kids needed it more than ever.

Of course, Ryder had no interest in auditioning for the play. In fact, when she suggested it to him, he shook his head. "I don't wanna be in any stupid play." Then, as if aware that his comment might have sounded disrespectful, he quickly added, "ma'am."

Paige didn't press the issue. She understood that some kids lived for the opportunity to get up on stage and others preferred to stay in the background. So she waited a couple of days, and then she casually mentioned that there was a lot of work to be done on the scenery for the play. Though he had a tendency to downplay his talent, Ryder was quite artistic. She didn't expect him to jump up and volunteer, and he didn't, but when she told him that she would appreciate any help he could give her on the project, he silently nodded his agreement.

While her days were busy with her students, Paige knew that Sutter was keeping busy, too. He was usually at the ranch, helping his father and his brothers with whatever needed to be done at the Triple T, but when he had time to spare, he made his way into town and invariably found somewhere else to lend a hand.

And whenever he was in town, he stopped by to see Paige before he headed home again. And the more time she spent with him, the more difficult it was to remember that they were only friends.

If she didn't see him every day, he called or texted. Sometimes more than once. She knew that she was playing a dangerous game, but every time she tried to put on the brakes or pull back, Sutter was there. And it would only take one stroke of a fingertip over the back of her hand or a casual brush of his lips against hers and she would forget all the reasons why getting involved again was a bad idea.

With each day that passed, Paige couldn't help but notice that everything seemed better when she was with Sutter. She'd thought she was perfectly content with her life, but with Sutter she was truly happy, and at the same time frustratingly discontented. Because every time he kissed her or touched her, he made her want *more*.

And as one day turned into the next, it got harder and harder for Paige to keep him at a distance. It didn't seem to matter that she knew it would be a mistake to get involved with Sutter again, that it was only a matter of time before he left Rust Creek Falls and headed back to Seattle.

Because the longer he stayed, the more she found herself hoping that he'd stay forever. She knew that wasn't a fair or reasonable hope when he had a business in Seattle, but still it blossomed inside her heart.

And if he asks you to go to Seattle with him again? Lindsay's words echoed in her mind, giving her pause. If he wouldn't stay—would she be willing to go? Her head cautioned against it, but her heart was quietly pounding, "Yes. Yes. Yes." But it was a moot question, because he hadn't asked her.

On Wednesday, Sutter spent the afternoon helping rebuild fences in town, so she invited him to come over for dinner when he was finished. Although he didn't show up at her place until almost seven o'clock, she was just pulling the chicken out of the oven.

"I was going to apologize for being late, but apparently I'm not."

"You are," she told him. "But I'm running behind schedule, too."

"Had to keep some unruly students after class?" he teased.

She just shook her head. "And I have to renege on our plans for tomorrow night."

"Why's that?"

"I have four pounds of ground beef that need to be made into meat loaves."

"You don't even like meat loaf."

She wondered how, after five years, he remembered that when her own mother never did. "It's for my mom," she admitted. "She was carrying a basket of laundry up the stairs and fell and broke her collarbone."

"Ouch," he said, reminding her that he'd suffered the same injury when he'd been thrown from a horse when he was thirteen. "That's not fun."

"No," she agreed. "That's why dinner's late—my dad was in court today so she called me, and I spent three hours at the clinic with her this afternoon."

"Is there anything I can do to help?"

She was touched that he would ask. Especially considering that neither of her parents had been warm or welcoming since his return. But Sutter had always been willing to lend a hand wherever it was needed, as evidenced by his return to Rust Creek Falls despite the tension that remained between him and his parents.

"Thanks, but my sisters have made a schedule of household chores and meal preparation. I'm on dinner prep Tuesdays and kitchen cleanup Thursdays. They've even got Caleb scheduled to do laundry, which makes me doubly grateful that I have my own washer and dryer."

"Are you scheduled for anything on Saturday?"

"Not officially," she told him. "But I'll probably be at the school for a few hours in the morning, and then I need to get started on my holiday baking."

"It's only the middle of November."

"It's not *only* but *already* the middle of November," she clarified. "And with my mom being laid up, I offered to do her baking, too."

"Do you want a few extra pairs of hands?"

She eyed him warily. "I'd say it depends on who those extra hands belong to."

"Me and my nephews."

"I can't quite picture you decorating sugar cookies."

"Well, if it was up to me, I'd show you a more creative

use of icing and sprinkles, but since I promised to take Dallas's boys for the day, that will have to wait."

The heat in his gaze practically singed her from the tips of her toes to the top of her head. And the slow, sexy smile that curved his lips made all of her female parts ache and throb. It was too easy to imagine what he was thinking, and now she was thinking it, too, and wishing that he wouldn't have the boys with him on Saturday.

"You should check with your nephews first," she told him.

"Why?"

"Because I get the impression that Ryder isn't too excited about the holidays."

"Probably because it was the day after Christmas last year that Laurel walked out," Sutter told her.

She hadn't been sure of the exact date, but she'd remembered that it had been sometime around Christmas because it had been a hot topic of conversation in town after the holidays—the fact that Dallas's wife had packed up and walked out, not just on her husband but her children.

Paige still didn't understand how Laurel could have done such a thing. Maybe she'd fallen out of love with her husband—and considering the man's grumpy attitude of late, Paige could understand how that might happen. But she didn't understand how any woman could abandon her children, and Paige's heart broke for the three beautiful boys who had been left behind.

"That would certainly explain his less than jolly attitude," she acknowledged.

"You didn't know?"

She shook her head. "Not any of the details."

"She didn't even talk to him about it," Sutter told her

now. "He just woke up on the morning of December 26 and found a note on her pillow."

"I heard it mentioned that one of the Triple T's ranch hands disappeared around the same time as Laurel."

"I heard the same thing, and if she fell in love with someone else, that might be some explanation for wanting out of her marriage. But whether it's true or not, I don't know. Dallas certainly never confided in me."

"At least she didn't try to take the boys."

"I'd like to think she knew she'd get one heck of a fight from the whole family if she tried, but the truth is, I don't think she wanted them."

"You don't think she's just waiting to get settled somewhere else before she comes back to get them?"

He shook his head. "My understanding is that the divorce papers gave full custody of the boys to Dallas."

"I don't get that—a woman walking away from her children."

And she knew that it wasn't an isolated case. In fact, Sutter's brother Clayton had experienced a similar situation. Although he hadn't been married to the mother of his child—in fact, he hadn't even known his girlfriend had been pregnant until Delia had showed up with the baby in her arms. And when Clayton had let her in the door, she'd dumped the baby in his lap and taken off, concerned about nothing so much as her own ambitions.

Clayton had lucked out, though, when he'd gone to Thunder Canyon and met Antonia Wright. Although she'd been pregnant with another man's baby when they met, the two had fallen in love and married, giving his son, Bennett, and her daughter, Lucy, a more traditional family.

She hoped, for his sake and that of his children, that Dallas would also find someone else to love. But she didn't hold out a lot of hope of that ever happening unless his surly attitude changed. In the meantime, she was pleased to know that the now-single dad was accepting the help that was offered by his family, because raising three active boys alone couldn't be easy.

"If you think the boys want to make cookies," she finally said to Sutter, "you can bring them over after lunch."

Sutter had just picked up the boys from Dallas's house when his cell phone rang. He recognized the number and immediately connected the call.

"I'm hands-free with kids in the car." He issued the warning because his friend's language was sometimes creative and colorful, and Sutter didn't want to have to explain to his brother the how or why if his kids went home with new words in their vocabulary.

"Kids? Heck, Sutter. You've been gone even longer than I realized."

"Funny, Reese. What's up?"

"Doug Barclay's been making noise—he's got Dancer's Destiny entered in the All American Stakes at Golden Gate Fields and he wants to discuss some concerns with you before then."

"I'll give him a call," Sutter promised.

"I got the impression that he wants to see you."

"Are there any problems with Dancer's Destiny?"

"Not that I'm aware of."

"Then I'll give him a call." He crossed over the Sawmill Street Bridge. "Was there anything else?"

"Yeah, we've got four more orders for custom-made saddles. I've sent the details to Collin."

"That's great," Sutter said. But he also knew it wasn't the type of news that warranted a phone call, especially if Reese had already been in contact with the new CT of CT Saddles.

"And I was wondering if you had any idea how much longer you were going to be in Rust Creek," Reese asked now.

"Not offhand."

"But the election's over, right?"

"The election's over," he confirmed. "And Collin's starting to settle in as the new mayor, but...some other issues have come up."

"All right," Reese finally said. "I'll tell Doug that you'll be in touch."

"Thanks. Hey, is Jenni there?"

"No." His friend responded to the question almost before Sutter had finished speaking. "She's, uh, she's in the arena, working with one of the yearlings."

"Okay. Tell her I'll catch up with her later."

"Sure."

Sutter had barely disconnected the call when Ryder said, "Who's Jenni?"

There was more than a bit of an edge to his voice that had all kinds of questions churning in Sutter's mind, but he only said, "She works at my stables in Seattle."

"Is she your girlfriend?"

"Ew—girls are gross," Robbie chimed in.

Sutter stifled a smile. "No," he said in response to Ryder's question. "Jenni isn't my girlfriend."

"Because Miss Dalton's your girlfriend, right?"

Suddenly he understood the edge to his eldest nephew's tone. Although Dallas had tried to keep the details of their mother's abandonment from the kids, Ryder had likely heard rumors about his mother having a boyfriend. And as much as he hated to label his relationship with Paige, especially in any way that put boundaries around it, he decided that, under the circumstances, it wasn't just wise but necessary.

"Miss Dalton and I have been friends for a long time," he informed his nephews.

"You sent her flowers," Ryder said, accusation in his tone.

"Did you kiss her?" Jake wanted to know.

"Ew," Robbie said again. "Kissing's gross."

"How do you know?" his brother challenged. "How many girls have you kissed?"

"None."

"Kissing is not gross," Sutter said. "Not when it's an expression of caring between two people who really like one another."

"Jake likes Mikayla," Robbie said.

"Do not," his brother denied hotly.

"Do, too."

"Do not."

"Boys!"

They immediately fell silent.

He pulled into Paige's driveway and shifted into Park, then he turned to face the three of them in the backseat.

"Girls are not gross and kissing is not gross, although when I was six, I probably thought so, too," he admitted to Robbie.

He shifted his gaze to Ryder. "Miss Dalton is not my girlfriend, although she used to be and I'm hoping that she might one day be again.

"But for today—" he looked from one to the other, including all of them now "—I would appreciate it if you put any other comments or questions on this topic on hold until the drive home."

And maybe by then he'd be one step closer to having Miss Dalton as his girlfriend again.

Chapter Ten

Paige had borrowed some aprons from the supply that Willa kept for her kindergarten class, and she made sure the boys were washed up and their clothes covered before she let them loose in the kitchen. She'd actually started baking the night before, making a couple dozen gingerbread cookies for Sutter's nephews to decorate. Those were in a plastic container in the cupboard, in reserve for when the boys got bored or tired of helping.

Robbie was, of course, totally enthused. He was on his knees on a stool at the island, digging a measuring cup into the bag of flour before Paige even had a chance to ask them what they wanted to make first. Jake headed straight for the bowl of minimarshmallows and immediately set about trying to figure out how many of them he could cram into his mouth. When he finally stopped gagging, he was thirsty from all the sugar, so Paige got him a glass of milk. Robbie decided that he needed a drink, too, but he wanted juice.

Ryder declined her offer of milk or juice with a polite, "No, thank you," then stood in the background, quietly waiting for instructions. She could tell that helping to bake cookies wouldn't make his top-ten list of favorite things to do—heck, it probably wouldn't make a list of the top one hundred—but he didn't protest.

She decided to put Ryder in charge of measuring the liquid ingredients because he was patient and meticulous and less likely to spill anything. Jake was assigned the task of measuring the dry ingredients, and Robbie got to wield the spoon and mix everything together.

"I thought you were going to help with this," Paige said to Sutter, who seemed content to stand back and watch the sloppily choreographed chaos in the kitchen.

"Absolutely," he agreed. "But my job doesn't start until the first batch comes out of the oven."

"What's your job?" Jake asked.

"Quality control."

"What's that?" Robbie wanted to know.

"It's a fancy term for someone who eats the cookies under the pretense of testing to see if they taste good," Paige informed him.

"I wanna be quality control," Robbie decided.

"Me, too," Jake agreed.

"Everyone will get to sample the cookies," she promised. "But we need to make them first."

They made a lot of cookies. And when they'd done as much as they could do, Paige got out the gingerbread cookies and various colored icings and decorations. The boys were each given half a dozen gingerbread cookies to decorate however they wanted. Ryder went heavy on the black icing, claiming that he was making ninja gingerbread men. Jake was more interested in eating than decorating. Robbie liked the colored sugars and holiday sprinkles and his philosophy was the more the merrier.

True to his word, Sutter worked quality control, sampling at least one of everything. But Paige didn't mind, because he didn't hesitate to lend a hand wherever it was required. He stood at the stove and melted marshmallows for the crisp-rice squares, dutifully chopped pecans for the thumbprint cookies and unwrapped dozens of cara-mels for the caramel nut bars.

When the boys were finished decorating, Paige gave them each a plate with a couple of cookies and a glass of milk. She didn't have a video-game system to occupy them, so they settled for watching a movie on television. Actually, Ryder played some game on his father's old cell phone in front of the television while his younger brothers watched the movie and Paige continued to work.

She still had peanut-butter bars and shortbread and lemon-snowdrop cookies to make, but she was happy with the progress she'd made today. She hadn't been sure if the extra hands Sutter had offered would be a help or a hindrance, and she suspected they'd been a little of both. But in the end, it didn't really matter because she'd sin-cerely enjoyed spending the afternoon with all of them.

Unfortunately, being with Sutter and his nephews made her think about the children she'd thought they would someday have together. She still wanted to get married and have a family, but she'd resigned herself to the fact that it wouldn't be with Sutter. Until spending time with him had that dream stirring again, and she knew that could be very dangerous. Because five years after Sutter had gone, she knew she still wasn't over him. She wondered if his coming back now and becom-ing friends would make it easier or harder for her when he went away again.

She rolled her head, trying to relieve the stiffness in her neck. Sutter settled his hands on her shoulders and began to knead the tight muscles. She moaned in sin-cere appreciation.

"Feel good?"

"Incredible," she admitted.

He dipped his head to whisper in her ear. "I could make you feel even better."

The husky promise in his voice had all her female parts standing at attention, but because she knew there was little chance of him following through, she managed to tease, "Right here and now?"

"Maybe not," he admitted, and sighed. "Are you ready to take a break?"

"I shouldn't," she said. "I still have so much to do."

"Ten minutes," he cajoled. "Come and sit down on the couch and watch the movie."

"Because nothing puts me in the holiday spirit like rampaging dinosaurs," she said drily.

She walked in at the scene where the brother and sister were hiding in the kitchen. She didn't particularly like scary movies, and although she agreed that the velociraptors were pretty low on the evil scale in comparison to knife-wielding psychopaths in goalie masks, she gasped out loud when one of the dinosaurs charged at the girl and crashed into a metal cabinet.

Ryder didn't look up from his screen. Jake glanced back at her and snickered, but Robbie climbed up on the couch beside her and snuggled close. Whether to offer her comfort or be comforted didn't matter to Paige. Within minutes, he was half-asleep with his head in her lap. She brushed a lock of hair off of his forehead. It was soft and silky, his cheeks were still round, his blue eyes—when they were open—still filled with innocence and wonder. Since the Traub genes weren't just evident but dominant in each of Dallas's sons, it was easy enough to imagine that Sutter's little boy might look very much like the one cuddled up against her. Robbie was fighting sleep, and perilously close to losing the battle until a roar from the screen had his eyes popping wide again. He shifted so that he was sitting up again, and stifled a yawn.

"Do you want me to see if I've got any books you might like better than this movie?"

He nodded.

Unfortunately she didn't really have anything age appropriate for a six-year-old, but she found some paper and crayons and sat him at the island to color while she cut and boxed up her goodies.

He'd drawn a couple of pictures—a boy on a horse, a house with a dad and three boys. But then he seemed to run out of ideas or interest.

"Do you want to do something else?" Paige asked him.

Robbie nodded. "Can you help me write a letter to Santa?"

"Absolutely." She closed up the box she'd finished packing, then sat down on the stool beside him.

"Dear Santa," he began, and she dutifully put the pen to fresh sheet of paper.

"I hope you had a good year and have lots of snow at the North Pole. Thanks for the presents you brung last year. I liked the dragon-lair building set best, but the pajamas were okay, too."

She fought back a smile as she carefully transcribed his words. But her smile faded at what came next, and an uncomfortable premonition filled her heart.

"This year for Christmas, I don't want any toys. Please bring my mommy home instead." He looked up when Paige stopped writing, his little brow furrowed. "You hafta write that."

Instead, she put the pen down and turned to face him. "I don't think Santa can bring her back, Robbie," she said gently.

"Even if I don't ask for nothin' else?"

"Unfortunately, only your mommy can decide if she wants to come back. I know you miss her, but—"

"I don't really miss her," he interjected, his tone matter-of-fact. "I just thought if she came home, Daddy wouldn't be sad anymore."

"How do you know your daddy's sad?"

"'Cuz he doesn't laugh anymore." He scraped at a drop of dried icing with his fingernail. "If Santa can't bring my mommy home, can he bring me a new mommy?"

"I think Santa's more accustomed to filling his sleigh with toys," she told him. "And the elves count on little boys and girls wanting toys, because it's their job to make them."

Robbie sighed. "Then I guess I wouldn't mind a deluxe neon alien-invasion spaceship."

After the movie was finished, Sutter packed up the boys—and the cookies that Paige insisted on sending home with them—and drove back to the Triple T. He considered returning to town, but he didn't want to push for too much too soon. He was confident that they would get to where he wanted to go. He just needed to be patient.

On the bright side, Sutter figured he was conserving electricity taking so many cold showers. In fact, he was just out of the shower, lounging on the couch with his feet up and a cold beer in his hand, when Dallas came in.

He gestured to the bottle his brother was holding. "Got another one of those?" he asked.

"Got several," Sutter told him. "Help yourself."

Dallas did, and settled into an oversize chair, his feet stretched out in front of him.

"The boys settled in for the night?"

"Just," Dallas told him. "They were so pumped up on sugar, I didn't think they were ever going to fall asleep."

Sutter lifted his bottle to his lips, drank deeply. "I suppose that's my fault?"

His brother just shrugged.

"They had a good time today, and if they were a little hyper when they got home, well, they're boys."

"That's what Mom said," Dallas admitted.

"You called in the cavalry?"

"She invited us up to the house for dinner."

As he knew she did every night. Ellie loved to cook for her sons and grandsons, and Sutter didn't blame his brother for taking her up on the offer. After working on the ranch all day, Sutter had enough trouble figuring out what he wanted to eat, never mind trying to feed three hungry—and picky—boys.

"What was for dinner?"

"Pork chops, scalloped potatoes, corn and mac and cheese."

Sutter's stomach growled.

"You could have come for dinner, too," Dallas told him. "I know Mom invited you."

And Sutter had declined, as he did almost every day. The one exception was Sunday lunch, when he knew there would be enough family members around the table to defuse the awkwardness. "She did. I already had other plans."

"With Paige?"

"With one of those handy microwavable trays that provides a complete meal, including dessert, in only a few minutes."

His brother wasn't sidetracked by his response. "It seems like you've picked back up with Paige Dalton again."

"Why does it sound as if you disapprove?"

Dallas shrugged. "It's not my place to approve or

disapprove—I'm just concerned that you don't realize you're wasting your time with her."

Sutter was more intrigued than annoyed by the statement. "How do you figure?"

"Because you keep telling everyone your life is in Seattle, and Paige is no more likely to leave Rust Creek Falls now than she was five years ago."

"A lot can change in five years," he told his brother.

Dallas was silent for a long minute before he finally said, "A lot can change in one year—and not always for the better."

"Paige isn't Laurel," Sutter pointed out.

"You're right—Laurel actually said yes when I asked her to marry me, and look how well that turned out."

Sutter frowned, not just at the bitterness in his brother's tone but at the blunt reminder that he'd proposed to Paige before he'd left town—and she'd turned him down. And yeah, that rejection had torn him apart at the time, but with some space and distance, he understood why she'd said no—and why it had probably been the right answer at that time.

Now, five years later, he hoped they would get to the point where he could ask the question again—and get a different answer this time. Because the more time he spent with Paige, the more time he wanted to spend with her. He wanted a life with her, a future, a family.

Watching her with his nephews today, he'd been more convinced than ever that she would be a fabulous mother. She hadn't been fazed by Robbie's exuberance, she hadn't flinched when Jake dropped a carton of eggs on the floor and she'd actually managed to tease a couple of smiles out of Ryder.

She'd been patient and attentive, and when she looked at him over a tray of unbaked and slightly mangled sugar cookies and smiled, he realized that he'd never fallen in love with another woman because he was still in love with Paige. And he didn't think it was too much of a stretch that she might still be in love with him, too.

Of course, she'd claimed to be in love with him five years ago, and—as Dallas had so kindly reminded him— she'd still turned down his proposal. She'd loved him then, but not enough to go to Seattle with him. And if she did still love him now, did she love him enough to give him a second chance? Did she love him enough to want a life with him, even if that life was outside of Rust Creek Falls?

"It's nothing against Paige personally," Dallas said now. "I just don't want you going through what I went through, and I can see you're heading in that direction."

"How do you figure?" Sutter challenged.

"You were high school sweethearts—just like me and Laurel. Everyone assumed you would get married some-day—just like me and Laurel. And when you proposed, you found out that you wanted to get married and she didn't."

"She never said she didn't want to marry me, she just didn't want to get married at that time and under those circumstances."

"The result was the same."

Sutter tried not to let his brother's comment rankle. He knew that Dallas was still smarting over his recent divorce and struggling to balance his responsibilities at the ranch with the demands of three young sons.

"Well, she didn't marry anyone else while I was gone," Sutter noted.

"Are you thinking she's changed her mind and will want to marry you now?" Dallas asked skeptically.

"I'm trying not to think too much and just enjoy the time we're spending together."

His brother shrugged and pushed himself to his feet. "Your time to waste," he decided, and dropped his empty beer bottle on the end table. "Since I can't find enough hours in a day, I better go. Thanks for taking the kids. And for the cookies."

"You should thank Paige for the cookies," Sutter pointed out.

"Yeah," his brother agreed, but they both knew he probably wouldn't go out of his way to do so.

The door closed behind Dallas, leaving Sutter alone with his thoughts again. He wondered about his brother's warnings, but he wasn't going to let Dallas's sour attitude dissuade him. Instead, he found himself thinking about Reese's unexpected phone call from earlier that day.

Sutter was in regular contact with his stable manager. In fact, he would guess that they probably exchanged no less than half a dozen text messages or emails on a daily basis. Which was why he'd been surprised to hear Reese's voice on the phone. The personal communication suggested to Sutter that there was more on his stable manager's mind than Doug Barclay's horse or Collin's saddles.

He felt a little guilty that he wasn't in Seattle to help with whatever Reese needed—but not guilty enough to be willing to leave Rust Creek Falls right now when he was finally making some progress with Paige. Not as much progress as he'd like, of course, considering his extremely high level of sexual frustration, but he was confident about the direction in which things were moving. And the kisses they'd shared reassured him that what he was feeling wasn't entirely one-sided.

But as much as he wanted Paige in his bed, he wanted more than just sex. He wanted a life with her. A future. A family. Unfortunately, there were still a lot of barriers to getting what he wanted. Even if Paige still loved him as much as he loved her, would that love be enough? It certainly didn't solve the problem of geography, and the more than five hundred miles that separated Rust Creek Falls from Seattle would definitely put the "long distance" in the relationship.

What he wanted—what he'd always wanted—was for Paige to choose to go to Seattle with him. But was it fair to expect her to leave her family, her friends and a job she obviously loved in order to start all over again in another city just to be with him? Maybe not, but he figured if she really loved him, she would be willing to do it.

With his brother's words echoing in the back of his mind, he accepted that even if she'd loved him five years ago, she hadn't loved him enough to make that choice. Was it foolish to hope that this time she might decide differently? That she might love him enough to give up her home and her job to build a new life with him?

And if he loved her enough, wouldn't he be willing to do the same?

He scowled at the idea of walking away from everything he'd built in Seattle. But the prospect of walking away from Paige was even more unthinkable.

Which meant that he had to figure out another option.

He picked up the phone and called Reese.

Chapter Eleven

Paige did some more baking after Sutter and the boys left, and when she finally fell into bed later that night, she was exhausted. And still she couldn't sleep. Despite the weariness of her body, her mind refused to stop churning. Because at some point between the crisp-rice squares and the caramel bars, she'd realized that she was still in love with Sutter.

She'd promised herself that she wouldn't fall in love with him again, that she wouldn't make the same mistake twice. And she hadn't. Because the truth was, she'd never stopped loving him.

Unfortunately, she knew that loving Sutter didn't miraculously make everything okay. There were still a lot of obstacles to overcome if they had any hope of maintaining a relationship and building a future together. The geographical distance was only one of those obstacles and, Paige feared, not even the most significant one.

A fact that was confirmed when she went to her parents' house after school on Monday to take her mother grocery shopping.

She didn't mind making the trip to Kalispell, but she was a little frustrated that her mother had been relying exclusively on her daughters for help since the accident that broke her collarbone. The traditional division of labor in her parents' home had never bothered her before, probably because her mother had willingly—and happily—performed all of the domestic chores.

But now that Mary's arm was in a sling, those duties had fallen to Lani, Lindsay and herself while Anderson, Travis and Caleb expected to show up for meals that would be ready and on the table with no effort on their parts. And God forbid any of them should actually pick up a dusting cloth or push the vacuum cleaner around, although Lani's schedule suggested that she hadn't given up hope.

Caleb had seemed willing to tackle the chore assigned to him, but he'd screwed up so badly with the washing machine he'd been permanently banned from the laundry room. He didn't seem overly disappointed about the banishment, making Paige suspect that his screwup had been deliberate.

"Heads up," Lindsay warned under her breath when she opened the door. "Mom heard that you broke up with Alex."

"Because of Sutter," Lani interjected.

Her tone made Paige suspect that her mother had probably heard the news from her sister, but she knew that didn't really matter. If she hadn't heard from Lani, she would have heard it somewhere else eventually, because nothing stayed a secret for very long in Rust Creek Falls. And she'd rather her mother know the truth than think that she was running around with Sutter behind Alex's back.

"It wasn't because of Sutter, and it was hardly a national secret," she informed both of her sisters.

But she was uneasy. Her mother didn't have strong opinions about a lot of things, but she'd clearly expressed her disapproval when Sutter spoke out against his brother's return to Iraq. And when Paige had started dating

Alex Monroe, Mary had been pleased by this "proof" that her eldest daughter was finally over her "silly infatuation" with "that Traub boy" and building a relationship with "a good man." Which meant that, regardless of the reason for the breakup of that relationship, Mary Dalton wasn't likely to be happy about it.

Throughout the drive to Kalispell, Paige kept waiting for her mother to say something about Alex or Sutter, but she seemed content to talk about other matters.

At the meat counter, they saw Carrie Reynolds—a friend of Paige's from high school who now lived and worked in Kalispell. Carrie fluttered her fingers in front of Paige to show off the diamond solitaire on her finger. After Paige had admired the ring and offered congratulations, Carrie said, "We're planning a June wedding. I really hope you can come. And Sutter, too, of course."

"I can only speak for myself," Paige said. "And I will be there."

"But you and Sutter are back together, aren't you?"

She shook her head.

Her friend frowned. "Really? Because I heard from Megan who heard from Rena that you're the reason he's back in Rust Creek Falls."

"Then somebody misheard something." Paige kept her voice neutral and deliberately did not look at her mother. "He came back because of the flood."

"But you've been spending a lot of time with him, haven't you?"

"I teach full-time and I've been helping with the reconstruction of the elementary school—I don't have a lot of time to spend anywhere else. In fact, I have tests I have to mark when I get home, so we should be going."

"Oh. Okay."

"But it was really good to see you," Paige told her. "And congratulations again."

"Thanks. And you should think about bringing Sutter to the wedding anyway. It's always more fun with a plus one."

Mary waited until they were back home and almost finished putting away the groceries before she said to Paige, "I didn't realize that Sutter was still in town."

"He is," she confirmed.

"Have you been out to the Triple T to see him?"

"Yes, I've been to the ranch, and he's been to my house."

Her mother didn't respond, but the thinning of her mouth was a sure sign of her disapproval, which Paige honestly didn't understand.

"You used to like Sutter," she reminded her.

"I did," Mary admitted begrudgingly. "Until he showed his true colors, and they weren't red, white and blue."

Paige sighed. "He didn't want his brother to go into a war zone and risk getting blown up. That doesn't make him unpatriotic, it just makes him human."

Her mother pursed her lips again. "The rest of the Traub family supported Forrest's decision, everyone except Sutter. And then he ran out on his family—and on you."

Paige could hardly claim that he hadn't run out on her when she'd accused Sutter of exactly the same thing. But she also realized that the situation hadn't been quite as black-and-white as she'd wanted to believe, and that she hadn't been an innocent victim. She'd made her choices as freely as he'd made his, and they were both responsible for the consequences.

"It was his choice to leave," she acknowledged now. "But only after he felt that everyone had turned their backs on him."

"He turned his back on his brother first, when all Forrest wanted to do was fight for his country."

"He was scared for his brother. Why can't you understand that?"

"If his brother wasn't afraid to go to war, then he should have been brave enough to support him."

"Because going back to Iraq turned out so well for Forrest," Paige said drily.

"He's a hero," Mary said firmly.

"I don't disagree," she said. "But his time overseas changed Forrest, and Sutter knew that if he went back, it would make things worse, not better."

"You think he somehow knew his brother's Humvee was going to get blown up?"

"I think he knew that Forrest would come home with scars."

"Last time I saw Forrest, he was getting along just fine. You can barely even notice the limp anymore."

"I'm not talking about the injury to his leg," Paige said. "I'm talking about the scars none of us can see— the ones that mark his heart and his soul."

"He seems happy enough with his new bride."

Clearly there was no way she was going to win this argument with her mother, though that didn't stop her from trying. "But it took him a long time to get there."

"And from what I've heard, with no help from his brother," Mary said. "What has Sutter done to mend their relationship?"

"I don't know," she admitted. "But I know he's changed. He's not the same man he was five years ago."

"And hopefully you're not the same woman," Mary said bluntly. "Because when he left, you cried for weeks."

"Yes, I cried," she admitted. "Because he wasn't just

my boyfriend, he was my best friend, and I didn't want him to go."

"I couldn't stand it if he hurt you like that again."

She sighed. "I know you only want what's best for me, but I'm twenty-seven years old—don't you think I know what's best for me?"

"Not if you think it's Sutter Traub," Mary said implacably.

Paige knew her mother meant well—honestly, she did—but that knowledge did nothing to stifle the urge to scream at her for being so completely unreasonable. Instead of screaming, she carefully folded the empty grocery bags and tucked them into the drawer reserved for that purpose.

"I really have to get home. I've still got those tests to mark for tomorrow."

"You're not going to stay for dinner?"

She shook her head. "I've got leftover meat loaf at home," she reminded her mother, then kissed her cheek.

"Call when you get home," Mary said, as she always did when her daughter headed out the door.

"I will," Paige confirmed, because it was easier to acquiesce than to remind her mother—for the thousandth time—that she lived less than a five-minute drive away.

Tonight that five-minute drive wasn't nearly long enough to diffuse her frustration, although Paige didn't know if she was more frustrated with her family or herself.

She was twenty-seven years old—she didn't need their approval. But they were her family, and she didn't like to be at odds with them over anything. The Dalton and Traub families had known one another forever and had always gotten along well. That hadn't changed when Sutter had left Rust Creek Falls. The only thing that had changed was that he had suddenly become an outcast, not just to her family but to the whole town, including his own.

Paige had never really understood how that had happened. She might not have agreed with Sutter's position regarding his brother's reenlistment, but she understood. If one of her brothers had decided to pick up and join the army during a war, she would be incredibly proud of him—and absolutely terrified *for* him. She would have felt all the same things that Sutter had felt, and she didn't like that he'd been made a scapegoat for daring to speak aloud what many others had been thinking and feeling.

She'd had words with Ellie Traub not long after Sutter had left town, when she'd crossed paths with Sutter's mother at the library. Those words played back in her mind now.

"Have you talked to Sutter?" Ellie's tone was hopeful, almost desperate.

Paige shook her head.

Disappointment had the other woman's eyes filling with tears. "I wish you'd gone with him. I hate knowing that he's so far away—and all alone."

It wasn't in Paige's nature to be disrespectful, and she loved Ellie like a second mother, but the unfairness of the statement demanded a response. "Well, I wish he hadn't left Rust Creek Falls at all," she said coolly. "But what choice did he have when his own mother told him he wasn't welcome in her home?"

"I didn't mean it like that," Ellie protested, and started to cry. "I never wanted him to go. I only wanted him to support his brother."

Of course, her tears had only made Paige feel worse. They'd ended up crying together—bound by their love for Sutter and their grief that he was gone—and they'd made their peace with one another. Unfortunately, Paige didn't know how to get her parents to make peace with Sutter's choices.

Part of it was her own fault. She knew her family was protective of her because Sutter had broken her heart. What should she have done—act as if it didn't matter that he'd left Rust Creek Falls? She'd never been very good at hiding her feelings, and there had been no way she could have pretended that he hadn't broken her heart wide-open.

Sutter was sitting on the top step of Paige's front porch when she got home. Her heart gave a little jolt when she saw him. She'd experienced a lot of those jolts lately, actual surges of emotion through her system that churned up everything inside. She'd seen him fairly regularly over the past couple of weeks, and she knew her reaction wasn't just the effect of his presence on her recently reawakened hormones, but a stronger and deeper yearning in her heart.

He smiled when he saw her, and his obvious pleasure made her feel all warm and tingly inside.

"What brings you into town tonight?"

"I needed some space."

"More space than you'd have tucked away in Clayton's house on an enormous ranch all by yourself?"

"Okay—maybe I wanted to see you more than I wanted space," he admitted. "Why do you look as if you're ready to spit nails?"

"Grocery shopping with my mother."

"I didn't realize you disliked shopping so much."

"I dislike being interrogated."

"About me," he guessed.

She nodded.

"I'm sorry."

"It's not your fault."

"I've been getting some grief from my family, too," he told her.

"About me?"

"Yeah. Since you came out to the ranch the night of the election, my mom's been wanting me to invite you to the Triple T for Sunday dinner."

"What did you tell her?"

"That meeting the parents is a big step, and I didn't want to rush into anything."

She smiled at that. "It is a big step—and it could send the wrong message."

"Ryder already asked if you were my girlfriend," he confided. "On the way to your place Saturday."

"What did you tell him?"

"That girls are yucky— Oh, wait. That's what Robbie said."

She smiled again. "Give him a few years. He'll change his mind. He's your nephew after all."

"Without a doubt," Sutter agreed.

"And he'll use those big blue eyes and trademark Traub smile to get exactly what he wants."

His lips curved, slowly, deliberately. "Does it work for me?"

"What do you want?" she asked warily.

"A cup of coffee?"

"I think that can be arranged."

The phone was ringing even as Paige slipped her key into the lock. She muttered under her breath as she pushed open the door and reached for the portable handset on the table in the hall.

"You said you would call when you got home," Mary said without preamble.

"I literally just walked through the door, Mom."

"Oh. Okay. Well, I just wanted to let you know that Lani is covering a shift for Courtney tonight, so on her way into work she's bringing over a piece of the pie that Lindsay made."

"I don't need any pie."

"You love pecan pie," Mary said, as if she needed reminding of the fact.

"Then you better send a big piece so I can share it."

"Are you expecting company?"

"As a matter of fact, Sutter's here."

She could almost see her mother's brow furrow. "He's there now?"

"Yes."

"You said you had tests to mark."

"I do, and I will get to that after I have a cup of coffee with a friend."

Mary was silent for a moment, and when she finally spoke she only said, "I hope it's decaf. You'll never get to sleep if you drink regular coffee this late in the day."

Paige closed her eyes and let her head fall back against the wall. "I'll talk to you tomorrow, okay?"

"Okay. I love you, Paige."

"I love you, too, Mom," she said, because she did.

Even if her mother frustrated her beyond belief at times.

Paige disconnected the call, then proceeded to the kitchen to make the promised coffee. Though she was acting as if the phone call hadn't bothered her, Sutter knew her too well to be fooled by the casual act. He also knew that Paige and her mother had always been close, and he didn't like knowing that he was the cause of any tension between them.

"Why did you tell your mother I was here?"

She finished measuring the grounds, then pressed the button to start the machine. "Was it supposed to be a secret?"

"No, I just didn't think you'd volunteer that information."

"We're not doing anything wrong—there's no reason to sneak around or for me to shove you into a closet when my sister comes to the door."

"Especially not with my truck parked out front," he noted wryly.

She shrugged. "We're friends, Sutter. I'm not ashamed of that fact."

"You're still on that friends kick, huh?"

"Because we are still friends," she said in a firm and decisive tone.

"Do you kiss all of your friends the way you kiss me?" he asked curiously.

Her cheeks flushed with color before she turned away to retrieve a couple of mugs from the cupboard. "Okay, so we're friends with some chemistry."

"Some *potent* chemistry, I'd say."

Before she could respond to that, the door opened and her sister walked in.

Lani dropped a plate on the counter and turned to Sutter. "Don't you live in Seattle now?"

"It's nice to see you, too, Lani," he said pleasantly.

Her gaze narrowed. "When are you going back?"

"I haven't quite decided yet."

Paige brought the two mugs to the island, passed one to him.

"Decide," Lani advised. "Soon."

"Lani," Paige said, a note of warning in her voice.

"If I didn't know better, I'd think you were trying to get rid of me," Sutter said to Lani.

"I am," she agreed unapologetically.

"You know what?" Paige interjected, her focus on her sister. "Sutter is a guest in my home. If you can't be nice to him, you can leave."

"I'm going," Lani said. "But only because I'll be late if I don't."

Paige sighed as the door closed again. "I'm sorry."

"No, *I'm* sorry," he told her. "I didn't realize how much your family would object to our...friendship."

She managed a smile.

"Maybe I should go back to Seattle," he said, almost to himself.

She lifted her cup to her lips, sipped. "If that's what you want."

Her tone was casual, but her refusal to look at him made him suspect that she wasn't as unconcerned about his decision as she wanted to appear.

"I don't want to cause any problems for you," he said.

"Don't make this about me."

"But it is about you," he insisted. "Or maybe it's about us."

"There is no us."

He didn't argue with her claim. In fact, he didn't say anything at all. Instead, he breached the short distance between them and covered her mouth with his own.

There was nothing tentative in his kiss this time. It was hot and demanding, and Paige was more than willing to meet his demands and counter with a few of her own. He'd always been a fabulous kisser. She'd kissed other men in the past five years, but no one had ever made her feel the way Sutter made her feel. No one else had created flutters in her belly, weakness in her knees or yearning in her heart.

She lifted her arms to link them behind his neck and

pressed her body close to his. His was so hard and strong, and every hormone in her body was jumping and dancing, begging for his attention. It had been a very long time since she'd felt this kind of desire, so sharp and fierce it was almost painful. And when he touched her, when his hands skimmed up her torso, barely brushing the sides of her breasts, she actually whimpered.

Desire pulsed in her veins, making her feel hot and weak, so hot she practically melted against him, so weak she needed his support to remain standing. His tongue delved between her lips, mated with hers in a slow, sensual seduction. His thumbs brushed over her nipples, making them pebble and ache, then circled around them, teasing and tempting. She arched against him, silently encouraging his exploration, urging him to touch, to take.

She wanted him. There was no point in denying it. But wanting and having were two very different things, and she knew it could be dangerous to indulge certain desires. Like on the rare occasions that she and her sisters went into Kalispell for brunch on a Saturday morning and she was tempted to order the mile-high chocolate cake instead of her usual spinach-and-cheese omelet. But of course, she never did. Because as much as she might want the decadent dessert, she knew it wasn't a suitable choice for breakfast. Sutter Traub was a lot more tempting than that luscious chocolate cake—and potentially much more dangerous to her heart. Not a suitable choice at all.

But still the only man she wanted.

He eased his mouth from hers. "There is, very definitely, an us," he told her.

Chapter Twelve

Paige wanted to believe that Sutter's feelings were as strong and deep as her own. But as she'd pointed out to him when he'd kissed her the night of the election, it didn't matter if he loved her or if she loved him—not so long as he wanted to be in Seattle and she wanted to stay in Rust Creek Falls.

She knew he couldn't run his business from Rust Creek Falls for the long-term, and he'd already been in town for more than four months with only brief and infrequent trips to Washington during that time. She was hopeful that his work at the Triple T with his dad and brothers would rekindle his interest in ranching and persuade him to sell his business in Seattle and move home for good. But was that a realistic possibility?

Whenever he talked about Traub Stables, she heard the pride in his voice, and she knew he was happy there. Maybe he could be happy ranching, too, but was it what he wanted? Or was it only what she wanted for him?

And even if he did stay, she knew it wouldn't work so long as there was tension within his family. Which meant that Paige had to talk to Ellie.

Monday night, after she'd done so, she called Sutter.

"Do you have any plans for dinner tomorrow?"

"Nothing specific, aside from eating," he said. "What were you thinking?"

"I was thinking you might enjoy a homemade meal at your place." She kept her tone light, deliberately casual.

"Am I cooking?"

She managed a laugh, because it seemed like an appropriate response and she didn't want him to suspect that her stomach was tied in knots. "No, you just have to show up."

"Then it sounds good to me. No, it sounds great to me."

Paige ignored the guilt that churned inside her. She didn't like misleading him, but she'd run out of other options. If Sutter and Ellie were ever going to bridge the gap between them, they needed a little shove toward the chasm. "Will you be at the ranch all day?"

"Actually, no. I'm going to be at Alistair Warren's place. He needs a hand to go through the boxes in his basement, to see if there's anything that can be salvaged."

"That sounds like an all-day job."

"He said there were only about a dozen boxes."

"And he'll have a story for every item and an anecdote about every scrap of paper," she warned him.

"Just tell me what time you want me to be home and I'll be there," he promised.

"Does six-thirty work?"

"Perfectly."

Paige had been right.

Alistair Warren had a story to go with every piece of junk in his basement, but Sutter didn't mind. The retired schoolteacher had never married, which meant that he had no children or grandchildren with whom to share the countless stories he'd amassed over seventy-four years. It also meant that what should have been a half-day job had taken the better part of a day, and still they weren't close to being finished.

Alistair held a bundle of water-stained letters in his gnarled hand. "Did you know I was engaged once?"

Sutter shook his head.

"Lizzie Carmichael was her name." The old man smiled a little at the memory. "We'd even set a wedding date. Then we got into an argument about something— honestly, I don't even remember what—and neither of us was willing to give in to the other."

He shook his head sadly. "She gave me back my ring, and I let her go. And I don't even remember why." Alistair tossed the damaged letters into the trash, then looked at Sutter. "Do you have a woman?"

"I'm working on it," he said, suddenly conscious of the late hour. "In fact, she's cooking dinner for me tonight."

"A local girl, then," Alistair noted. "Does that mean you plan on moving back to Rust Creek Falls?"

"I haven't made any firm plans."

"Women like a man to have a plan," the old bachelor told him. "So you'd better make one, otherwise you'll end up old and alone like me."

"Right now, my plan is not to be late," Sutter told him.

"What time is she expecting you?"

"Six-thirty."

"Then you'd better be on your way," Alistair advised.

Sutter nodded. "Do you want me to come back tomorrow to help finish this up?"

The old man seemed surprised by his offer. "If you don't have anything better to do, that would be appreciated."

"I'll see you tomorrow," he promised.

Twenty minutes later, he pulled into the driveway of Clayton's house. He felt a quick pang of disappointment when he didn't see Paige's car, but when he walked in the back door, he immediately recognized the scent of his favorite buttermilk-fried chicken.

He smiled at the thought that Paige had cajoled the recipe from his mother for the occasion. The smile faded when he realized that it wasn't Paige standing by the stove—but his mother.

"She set me up."

He hadn't intended to speak the words aloud—and didn't realize he had until he saw Ellie's tentative smile wobble.

"It was my idea," she said quickly.

"I doubt that." If Ellie had wanted to ambush him, she would have done so weeks earlier. The fact that she'd done so only now, after Paige had insisted he needed to talk to his mother and work things out, proved that her meddling fingerprints were all over this plan. And he wasn't entirely sure how he felt about that.

The flush that colored his mother's cheeks further confirmed his suspicions. "I just wanted a chance to talk to you, to say…"

"What did you want to say?"

His mother's eyes filled with tears. "That I'm sorry."

And that quickly, he felt the shell around his heart begin to crack, just a little.

"While I was waiting for you, I was trying to figure out what I would say," she admitted. "How to tell you everything I've been thinking and feeling, how much the regrets have weighed heavy in my heart for the past five years. I had a speech prepared, but I can't remember any of it now. All I can tell you is that I'm so sorry." Despite the tears that spilled onto her cheeks, her gaze didn't waver. "I know I was responsible for your decision to leave, but I never wanted you to go."

Leaving hadn't been his choice so much as a necessity at the time, and he'd been an outcast from his family for five years because harsh words had been spoken and difficult decisions had been made. But over the years, he'd realized that he bore as much responsibility as anyone else for those words and decisions, and if his mother was brave enough to take the first step toward bridging the gap between them, then he could at least meet her halfway.

He took three steps toward her and opened his arms. Though her eyes were still swimming with tears, he saw the quick flare of hope and then she was in his arms, holding on to him and sobbing against his shirt.

"I'm sorry, too," he said, when her sobs had finally subsided.

She pulled herself from his embrace and tried to wipe the tears from her cheeks, but they wouldn't stop falling. "Why are you sorry?"

"Because I was too proud and stubborn to come home when I wanted to."

She cupped his face in her hands. "Those are traits you come by honestly enough. Just like loyalty, which brought you home when we needed you."

"When I heard about the flood—I was so worried about the ranch, about all of you."

"I can't tell you what it meant to me to see your truck in the driveway that first day you came back—to know that you'd finally come home."

He remembered the smile that had spread across her face—and how quickly it had disappeared when he'd pointedly reminded her that his home was in Seattle now, and that he would stay at Clayton's house while he was in town to help out, so long as they needed help.

"I understand why you chose to stay here," she told

him now. "I didn't like it, but I understood. And knowing that you were just a few minutes up the road was so much better than you being in a different state.

"But if you want to move your things back to the main house, you're welcome to do so. Your room is just the way you left it— Well, I picked up some things you left lying around, and I've cleaned and vacuumed a few times since you've been gone, but it's mostly the same."

He smiled at that. "Thanks, but I'm not sure how I'd feel about living with Mom and Dad again—even temporarily—after being on my own for five years."

She nodded. "I guess I can understand why you'd want the privacy here, especially now that you and Paige are back together."

Was she only repeating what she'd heard around town, or had Paige given some indication that they were heading in that direction? "What makes you say that?" he asked cautiously.

"I guess I just assumed… You've been seeing a lot of her, and…"

"And she set this up," he said again.

"She thought it was important for us to talk," Ellie said.

"She was right."

"She obviously still cares about you."

He didn't know if it was obvious, but he hoped it was true. And as grateful as he was that Paige had helped him bridge the gap with his mother, that didn't mean he was going to confess his deepest feelings to her. Instead, he gestured to the oven. "Is that fried chicken in there?"

She nodded. "And roasted potatoes, buttered carrots and corn bread."

All of his favorites.

"Are you hungry?" Ellie asked hopefully.

"Famished," he told her.

She smiled. "Let's eat."

While Sutter was having dinner with his mother, Paige was pacing her kitchen, unable to choke down a single mouthful of the grilled tilapia and rice that she'd prepared for her own dinner. It was seven o'clock, so she knew that he would have arrived home by now—and found Ellie preparing his meal.

Paige knew that Sutter's mother had some reservations about what she considered to be an ambush, but she would be there. She loved her son too much not to do whatever was necessary to bring him fully back into the fold of her family.

Paige was confident that Ellie could handle it because she knew what was coming. Sutter, on the other hand, had no clue, and she didn't know how he would respond. It was entirely possible that he would be furious with both her and his mother.

She picked at her now-cold fish, managed a couple of forkfuls of rice before she dumped the rest of it in the garbage. She tidied up the kitchen, then she dusted and vacuumed her living room/classroom, and when a knock sounded on the front door, she nearly jumped out of her skin.

She peeked through the front window and recognized Sutter's truck. Her knees were trembling as she made her way to the door, and her heart was lodged in her throat so that she wasn't sure she'd be able to speak past it. But it didn't matter, because Sutter didn't wait for an invitation, walking right into the house when she opened the door for him.

Because her living room was still a classroom, he took a seat at the kitchen island.

Paige leaned back against the counter, facing him.

"Are you mad?"

"About what?"

Neither his tone nor his words gave away anything of what he was thinking or feeling. "About dinner tonight," she prompted.

"Why would I be mad?" he said easily. "No one makes fried chicken like my mother."

"You're deliberately misunderstanding me."

"So this isn't one of those times when you want me to misunderstand you?"

She felt her cheeks flush. "Okay—I should learn to mind my own business."

"That was my first thought when I walked into the house and found my mother in the kitchen instead of you," he admitted.

"Do you want me to apologize?"

"No." He pushed off the stool and rounded the island to stand in front of her. "I want to know why."

She wasn't ready to admit that she'd hoped if he worked things out with his family, he might think about moving back to Rust Creek Falls. "Because I don't know when to mind my own business?" she suggested instead.

"Maybe," he acknowledged. "And I guess the reason doesn't matter as much as the result."

She exhaled slowly, "Does that mean you talked?"

"Yes, we talked, we hugged, she cried. It was just like a made-for-TV movie."

The curve of her lips was probably just a little smug.

"You're dying to say 'I told you so,' aren't you?" Sutter noted.

"No," she denied. "Actually I'm just marveling over the fact that you're talking about your feelings—and still breathing."

He lowered his head toward her. "If I stop breathing, will you give me mouth-to-mouth?"

"I don't think you need to worry."

"Maybe we should take some preemptive measures—" he brushed his lips against hers "—just in case."

"Well, it's better to be safe than sorry, isn't it?"

"Absolutely." His fingers combed through the ends of her hair, tugging gently to tip her head back so that he could capture her mouth more completely.

His tongue delved between her lips, tangled with hers. Desire, hot and heavy, flooded her system, pulsed between her thighs. Her body quivered like a racehorse at the starting gate, eager to finally end three seemingly endless years of celibacy.

Except her mind wasn't nearly as ready as her body to forgive and forget and get naked. So when his hands skimmed down her back and over her buttocks and she was very close to melting into a puddle at his feet, she forced herself to pull away instead.

"What are we doing here, Sutter?"

"Well, I don't know about you, but I was hoping to get to second base," he teased.

She managed a smile. "Okay, but beyond the obvious. Why? Why are we going back down a road that's only going to lead to a dead end?"

"How do you know that it will?"

"Because nothing has really changed. Aside from your relationship with your mother, which is great, but somehow I don't think you've suddenly changed your mind about going back to Seattle."

"Can't we just enjoy the journey without worrying about the destination?"

"Maybe you can," she said. "But I can't. Because one trip to Heartbreak Falls was enough for me."

"You weren't the only one who was hurt," he reminded her.

"I know. So why would we want to go through that again?"

"Because we're not the same people we were five years ago, and I think—*I know*—things can be different this time."

She wanted to believe him, because she didn't want anything else as much as she wanted to be with him, but she wasn't quite ready to take that risk.

"Maybe they can," she finally allowed. "But one thing that hasn't changed is that Tuesday is still a school night."

"And you have a field trip planned with your class tomorrow," he remembered.

She nodded. "We're going to town hall to sort and organize the boxes and cans that have been collected so far for the community food drive."

"Maybe I'll stop by to help."

"We could use it," she told him. "Nina's done a great job promoting the food and clothing drives, and donations have been pretty steady."

The shopkeeper also planned to put up a "Tree of Hope" in the store after Thanksgiving and decorate it with tags for disadvantaged children. Her hope was that customers would choose tags, buy gifts for the children represented then return to the store with the gifts, which would be distributed to the children for Christmas. This community spirit that inspired even those who had lost so much to dig deep and find something to give to others less fortunate was yet another facet of the town that Paige loved.

"Then I'll see you tomorrow," he said, and brushed one last kiss on her lips before heading for the door.

* * *

Sutter had always known that family was important to Paige. If he'd had any doubts, the lengths to which she'd gone to ensure his reconciliation with his mother obliterated them. But he still hadn't fixed things with his brother, and he knew that was the necessary next step, because his breakup with Paige went back to his falling out with Forrest.

He'd wanted Paige to stand by him, to support him, but she'd sided with his brother instead. Or so it had seemed when he'd been twenty-three years old and had desperately needed someone to be on his side. In retrospect, he could accept that there had been no right or wrong, and that nothing that had been said or done then could have fixed what had gone wrong between him and his brother. Only he could do that.

And he needed to do it. Because fixing what was broken between him and Forrest was the only hope he had of fixing things with Paige for good. And he wanted to fix things with Paige, because she was the only woman he'd ever loved—and the woman he still loved.

He knew that she still had strong feelings for him, too, but she was wary. He understood why. The frequent references she made to his life in Seattle were proof that she expected him to leave again—because he'd told her that he would. But that conversation had taken place before the election, and a lot had changed in the weeks that had passed since then.

This wasn't his first trip back to Rust Creek Falls since he'd left town five years earlier, but he could count the number of trips on one hand, and every one of his previous trips had been of short duration. In fact, prior to this most recent visit, he didn't think he'd ever managed to stay longer than a weekend. Even when he'd planned to spend a week or two, old hurts and insecurities had reared up and driven him back to Seattle again.

He was determined to finally put those old hurts and insecurities to rest so that he could look to the future instead of the past. He knew that Forrest and Angie were in Rust Creek Falls for Thanksgiving, and he knew he couldn't delay any longer. Before Forrest had enlisted, when he'd thought he would stay in Rust Creek Falls and work on the Triple T with his father and his brothers, he'd built a small house on the property. Since Sutter didn't want to cause a scene in front of the whole family, he decided to track his brother down there.

Despite the chill in the air, Sutter felt perspiration bead on his brow as he approached the front door. Now that he was actually at the door of his brother's house, his heart was pounding in his chest and his mind was assailed by doubts and fears, the foremost one being: What if Forrest turned him away?

And he realized it was the fear of screwing up again that had held him back from making any overture prior to now. So long as he hadn't reached out and been slapped back, there was always the possibility of fixing his relationship with Forrest. But if he tried and failed— No, he didn't even want to consider the possibility.

He was relieved when the door opened and he saw that it wasn't Forrest standing on the other side but his beautiful young wife, Angie.

"Sutter?"

He couldn't blame her for being uncertain—they'd only met once before, when she and Forrest had come to Rust Creek Falls the night of the election to support Collin in his bid for mayor.

"Yeah," he said. "I apologize for dropping by uninvited—"

"You're family," she interjected, and a smile of genuine pleasure and welcome spread across her face. "Family doesn't need an invitation. Please come in."

Sutter stepped inside, and removed his hat from his head.

"Can I get you anything? A cup of coffee?" She glanced pointedly at the hands that clutched the brim of his hat. "A glass of whiskey?"

So much for thinking he didn't look as nervous as he felt. He cleared his throat. "Actually, coffee would be great, if it's not too much trouble."

"It's already on," she said, leading him back to the kitchen.

She gestured for him to sit, so he did, and she poured a fresh mug of coffee for him.

"Is, uh, Forrest around?"

"He just went out for a walk—part of his morning ritual. The exercise helps ease the stiffness in his leg and the fresh air helps clear his head. He still has nightmares sometimes," she confided, "but not as often as he used to."

"Forrest and I— We've never really talked about what he went through in Iraq," he admitted.

"Probably because you've barely spoken at all since he got back."

"He told you that?"

"He did," she confirmed, and the look she sent him was almost apologetic. "And so has everyone else in town."

"I should have figured."

Angie reached across the table and touched his hand. "But you're here now, and that's what matters."

"I guess we'll have to see if your husband shares that opinion."

As if on cue, the back door opened and Forrest came in.

"Sutter." Forrest looked from his brother to Angie, as if she might have the answers to the questions that were undoubtedly spinning through his mind.

"I hope it's okay that I stopped by."

"Sure. I'm just…surprised." He looked at his wife again, silently—almost desperately—pleading.

Angie poured another mug of coffee and pressed it into Forrest's hands. "I'm going to head up to the main house, to see if your mom needs anything from town," she said.

Then she kissed her husband, and gently squeezed Sutter's shoulder as she passed.

Forrest didn't move until the door closed behind her, then he took a couple of hesitant steps toward the table and finally lowered himself into a chair across from his brother.

"It looks like the move to Thunder Canyon was a good one for you," Sutter noted.

The hint of a smile played around the corners of his brother's mouth. "Better than good."

"Marriage definitely agrees with you."

"I didn't think it was what I wanted," Forrest told him. "After Iraq, I was so messed up. I felt guilty for living when so many others had died. And I didn't want to be happy. I didn't think I deserved to be happy. Then I met Angie."

"And put a ring on her finger before she could change her mind?" he teased.

"Angie was the one who was in a hurry. I just wanted to make her happy." He took his time sipping his coffee, as if he was trying to figure out what else to say. "You could've come to the wedding."

"I did," Sutter admitted.

Forrest frowned. "You were there?"

Sutter nodded. "But I didn't want anyone to know I was there, so I snuck in the back of the church just as the bride was starting to walk down the aisle. By the way, interesting choice of ring bearer."

His brother inclined his head. "Apparently you *were* there."

"I'm guessing there's a story behind the dog?"

Forrest nodded. "Smiley's a therapy dog—and the reason I met Angie."

"You looked happy," Sutter said.

"I've never been happier," his brother said. "Angie wasn't just what I wanted, but what I needed. She turned my life around."

"I'm glad." He finished his coffee and decided he'd procrastinated long enough. "But I didn't come here to talk about your wedding."

"I didn't think you did."

"I wanted to talk to you… Well, I guess I just really needed to say that…I'm sorry."

"What exactly are you apologizing for?"

"For not supporting you when you chose to go back to Iraq."

"You were expressing your opinion." His gaze dropped to his leg. "And it turned out you were right to have some concerns."

"I didn't want to be right," Sutter told him. "I just wanted you to be safe. I was terrified that something would happen and I'd lose you forever." He dropped his gaze to the now-empty mug he held cradled between his palms so that he could pretend his eyes weren't blurred with tears.

"And thank God you came home and we didn't lose you forever," he continued, when he was sure he could do so without blubbering. "But the past five years have felt like forever. And I hope you can forgive me, because I'd really like my brother back."

Forrest cleared his throat. "I'd like mine back, too."

"Really?" Sutter couldn't believe his brother was letting him off the hook so easily. Except that if he considered that he'd been estranged from most of his family and Forrest had nearly been killed, none of it had been easy for either of them.

"Really," Forrest confirmed.

"Now I wish I'd had the courage to initiate this conversation when you'd first returned from Iraq."

His brother shook his head. "I wasn't ready then, and not for a long time after. Probably not until Angie pushed her way into my life."

"I'm looking forward to getting to know her and hearing her version of the story," Sutter said.

"She taught me not to live in the past," Forrest confided. "And she gave me hope for the kind of future I long ago gave up thinking I could ever have."

"I guess when you have a woman like that, you'd be crazy to let her go."

"You're thinking about Paige," his brother guessed.

Sutter nodded. "I made a lot of mistakes five years ago."

"Is she still making you pay for them?"

"No. Yes." He shook his head. "I don't even know. She doesn't seem to be holding a grudge, but she is holding back."

"You want more than she's giving you?"

"I want it all," Sutter admitted.

Forrest's brows lifted in silent question.

"Marriage, kids, forever," he clarified.

"Have you told her that?"

"Not yet."

"What are you waiting for?"

He wasn't sure. Or maybe he was worried that Paige wasn't sure. And he wasn't ready to put his heart on the line without being certain that hers was involved, too.

"If I learned nothing else in Iraq, I learned that there are no guaranteed tomorrows. If you want to be with Paige, don't wait to tell her."

Chapter Thirteen

Sutter invited Paige to Thanksgiving dinner at his parents' house, but she had to decline the invitation because her family was having their meal at the same time. When they'd dated in the past, they'd managed to get two meals out of the day because his family always had theirs at lunch and her family preferred to eat at dinnertime. But for some inexplicable reason that seemed to surprise Paige as much as it surprised him, Mary Dalton decided to have an early meal this year. Sutter half suspected that she'd deliberately scheduled her lunch to conflict with his family's plans and ensure that Paige wouldn't be able to spend the holiday with him.

His mother was bustling around the kitchen, completely in her element as she choreographed the preparations. Willa was mixing the coleslaw; Angie was mashing potatoes. Even Dallas's boys had been put to work: Ryder was putting pickles into trays, Jake was dumping dinner rolls into baskets and Robbie was helping his grandfather set the table.

When everything was ready and bowls and platters covered almost every inch of the table, they all sat down and Bob said grace. As the food was passed around, Ellie decided that—in honor of Thanksgiving—everyone should share something for which he or she was thankful. There were some subtle groans and protests, but his mother wasn't easily dissuaded.

"I'll start," she said as she added a spoonful of candied yams to her plate. "I'm thankful to Hank Pritchard for making the extension for this dining room table, but I'm especially grateful that so many of our children and grandchildren are here to sit around it with us today."

The only one of Sutter's siblings who hadn't come home for the holiday was Clayton. Sutter knew that his brother would have liked to have been there, but now he and Antonia were married and living on her family's ranch, where she managed the Wright Way boarding house with her widowed father and three brothers. And while Ellie was undoubtedly disappointed, she understood that Antonia had a family of her own and other responsibilities. That fact—along with Antonia's promise that they would come to Rust Creek Falls for Christmas—lessened her disappointment, at least a little.

Ellie looked at Robbie, who was seated to her left. "What are you thankful for?" she asked her grandson.

"That Uncle Collin married my teacher, 'cuz she smells really good."

Willa's cheeks flushed in response to the boy's exuberant comment while the other adults chuckled.

"I'm glad it's a long weekend, so there's no school until Monday," Jake declared.

"Braden?" Ellie prompted.

"This one's easy," he said. "I'm thankful that Sutter's home to help me muck out stalls."

Bob was up next, and he smiled at his wife at the opposite end of the long table. "I'm grateful that, forty years ago, I had the good sense to marry my Ellie."

Ellie's eyes sparkled with moisture as her own lips curved.

Angie was beside her father-in-law. "I'm thankful for my new husband and his wonderful family."

"I'm thankful for the support of my whole family—" Forrest looked at Sutter, then shifted his attention to his wife "—and especially for my beautiful wife."

The only one who faltered was Dallas, and Sutter could understand why he might not be feeling particularly thankful after the events of the past year. But when he finally spoke, he said, "I'm thankful for my sons— Ryder, Jake and Robbie—who are the very best part of my life."

Ellie's eyes filled with tears again. They all knew it had been a rough year for Dallas, and Sutter was glad his brother was able to appreciate how fortunate he was to have the three boys who looked at him as if he was the center of their world—and he was.

When it was finally Sutter's turn, he looked around the table, at the family he'd stayed away from for far too long, his gaze pausing on Forrest beside his new wife. "I'm thankful for the second chances that I've been given since returning to Rust Creek Falls."

Of course, thinking of second chances made him think of Paige, and the advice that his brother had given to him the day before. *There are no guaranteed tomorrows. If you want to be with Paige, don't wait to tell her.*

He'd barely touched the plate he'd heaped with the food his mother had spent hours preparing, but he pushed his chair away from the table and stood up.

Ellie looked at him, obviously startled—and not at all pleased—by his abrupt action. "What are you doing?"

"I have to see Paige."

She frowned. *"Now?"*

"Right now," Sutter confirmed. "Because she gave me a second chance, too, and I'm not going to blow it."

"I hardly think staying to finish your meal would blow anything," she chided.

Sutter looked at Forrest again. "I'm not willing to wait another minute to tell her how I feel about her."

Paige had always loved Thanksgiving, but as she sat at the dining room table with her family, she couldn't help feeling as if something—or some*one*—was missing. She wished Sutter was there, or that she was at the Triple T with his family. But with each of their families deciding to have the meal at similar times, there was no way for them to be together without choosing one over the other.

But maybe it was better this way. Maybe they needed to spend the holiday apart so that she would remember they had separate lives now. Lately she'd started to fall into the trap of thinking they were a couple again, because they'd been acting like a couple. Spending almost all of their free time together, talking every day when they couldn't see each other.

Every time her phone buzzed to indicate a text message, her heart started to beat just a little bit faster because it *might* be a message from Sutter. And if it was, she'd inevitably feel a smile steal across her face. She was acting like a lovesick teenager, further proof that she'd fallen for him all over again.

Paige and her sisters had just started clearing away the empty plates when there was a knock at the door. Visitors on Thanksgiving were unusual, as most everyone in town was celebrating the occasion with their own families. Since Paige was closest to the door, she responded to the knock—and her heart knocked hard against her ribs when she found Sutter on the porch.

He smiled. "Happy Thanksgiving."

"It is now," she said.

"Am I interrupting?"

"We just finished eating. Did you want to come in for dessert?"

He shook his head. "I just wanted to talk to you."

"Sounds ominous," she teased.

"It's not," he promised. "At least, I don't think it is."

"Then it can wait until after we have pie," she said, and took his hand to drag him into the dining room.

"We've got one more for dessert," she said brightly, dragging Sutter into the dining room.

There had been several conversations taking place around the table, and they all faded away.

"Happy Thanksgiving," Sutter said.

The chorus of halfhearted and mumbled responses immediately put Paige's back up. She understood that her family disapproved of certain things Sutter had said and done five years earlier, but if she'd gotten over them, she expected they should be able to do the same.

"I hope I'm not intruding," he said.

If he'd been anyone else—or if the same scene had played out more than five years earlier—her mother would have assured him that he wasn't and her father would have jumped up to find him a chair. Today, her mother only said, "I'm surprised to see you, Sutter. Doesn't Ellie usually host a big lunchtime meal on Thanksgiving?"

"Yes, she does. And she is," he told her. "But I slipped out early to see Paige."

"I imagine it was probably a little awkward around the table," Mary said, with false sympathy, "since your brother's home from Thunder Canyon for the holiday."

"Forrest and Angie are home, but Clay and Antonia stayed in Thunder Canyon," he clarified. "And no, it wasn't awkward at all."

"This, on the other hand, is starting to feel more than

a little uncomfortable," Paige noted. "Can't you be gracious and welcoming to a guest I've invited to join us?"

"There really isn't room for another chair at the table," her mother said primly.

Paige was stunned, as much by the dismissive tone as the blatant lie. "We've never had trouble squeezing in one more in the past."

"I didn't put the extra leaf in the table this year," Ben spoke up in support of his wife.

Her brothers, who had always been friendly with the Traub boys, said nothing. Paige wasn't sure if their silence was a deliberate decision to remain neutral or a result of the fact that they were too focused on their dessert to care about the conversation. Her sisters—especially Lani—*always* had something to say, but even they were quiet. And while Paige would have appreciated *some* support for Sutter from their corner, at least they hadn't joined the fray against him.

Paige had to take a deep breath before she could speak again. "Then I'm sure you'll all appreciate the extra elbow room since I'm not staying for dessert."

"Don't," Sutter said, touching her arm. "I didn't come over here to cause a scene."

"And *you* didn't," Paige assured him. Then, to her family, she said, "Happy Thanksgiving."

Ben scowled. "You can't just leave."

"Actually, I can. And right now, I think it's better that I do." Then she turned and walked out the door before she said something she knew she would regret.

"I'm sorry," Sutter said, when he led her to his vehicle.

"Why are you sorry?"

He opened the passenger door for her, helped her up. "Because I put you in an awkward position by showing up the way I did."

She shook her head. "I'm glad you came by."

"You're glad I caused dissension between you and your family?"

"You didn't cause it," she denied. "They did."

He went around to his side and climbed in. "They're your family, Paige. And I know, probably better than anyone, how hard it is to be at odds with family."

She nodded. "You're right. But aside from the fact that they're being completely unfair, they have to stop trying to control my life and my choices."

"Are you choosing to be with me?"

"It seems that, at least for today, I am."

"What about tomorrow?"

"I don't know," she admitted. "Right now I'm afraid to look too far ahead, because when I do, I see you back in Seattle."

"My business is in Seattle," he agreed. "Not my life."

She felt hope swell inside of her chest. "When did you come to this realization?"

"Sometime between the night of the election, when I kissed you as the snow fell around us, and yesterday, when I was talking to my brother."

She didn't need to ask—she could tell by the tone of his voice that he meant Forrest. "How did that go?"

"Much better than I expected."

She reached for his hand, squeezed it. "I'm so glad."

"Me, too. And one of the things I decided after talking to Forrest was that I wasn't going to waste any time going after what I wanted."

"And you wanted...me?"

"I've always wanted you," Sutter told her. "Even when I was five hundred miles away, I wanted you. Even after five years, I never stopped."

Wow—that was a declaration she hadn't expected.

And she didn't quite know how to respond. She could tell him that she felt the same way, because it was true. But she was wary about opening her heart so completely when she wasn't sure that there was a future for them, and if there wasn't, he would break her heart all over again.

On the other hand, he'd taken the first step in coming to her tonight—he'd stood firm despite the disapproval of her family and he'd put his feelings on the line. He hadn't professed undying love or promised her forever, but she wouldn't have trusted either of those claims if he had. She'd been in love with Sutter before and she knew there were no guarantees. What he was offering her now was honest and real, and she wasn't going to turn him away.

He pulled into her driveway, put the vehicle into Park. She waited for him to turn off the ignition, but he didn't. She looked at him, silently questioning.

"I'm waiting to see if you're going to invite me to come inside," he told her.

It seemed like a simple response, but she somehow sensed that there would be no going back if they went forward from here. She could go into the house alone and he would drive away. Or—

She drew in a deep breath. "Would you like to come inside?"

He turned off the ignition.

Paige led him into the house. Now that they were inside, alone, she suddenly felt nervous. It wasn't the first time she'd invited him into her home, but it was different this time because they both knew he wouldn't be leaving tonight.

"Can I get you anything? Beer? Soda? Water?"

Sutter shook his head. "No, thanks."

She took a glass from the cupboard and filled it with water, more because she needed something to do than because she was thirsty. She took a few sips and tried to put her scattered thoughts into some semblance of order.

He pried the glass from her fingers and set it on the counter, then he put his arms around her and drew her close. "I can almost hear you thinking, but I don't have a clue what's going through your mind."

"I'm not sure I do, either," she admitted. "I guess I'm just wondering, when you said you wanted me, did you just mean for tonight? Or are you planning to stay in Rust Creek Falls?"

"I haven't made any firm plans yet, but I'm hoping to stay here—with you." He brushed his lips against hers. "If you want me to stay."

"I want you to stay," she said, and kissed him again.

She was sure there were more questions she should ask, but right now she couldn't think of any of them. She couldn't think of anything while he was holding her and kissing her, except how much she wanted to be with him.

"Is your mother going to wonder if you made it home safely?"

Paige sighed. "She might."

"Why don't you give her a call to preempt any interruptions?"

She did so, and was grateful that Travis answered so she could leave the simple message and hang up. Then she turned back to Sutter.

"No more interruptions," she promised and, taking his hand, led him upstairs to her bedroom.

"This is the second time you've brought me up here— I hope you know what you're doing this time."

"I know exactly what I'm doing...and who I'm doing it with," she said, and brought his mouth down to hers.

She might have initiated the kiss, but he was an avid and equal participant. He kissed her again, deeply, hungrily. She pressed closer so that her breasts were crushed against his chest and the rock-hard evidence of his arousal was against her belly. Desire pounded through her veins, pulsed deep inside her.

His hands slipped under her sweater, and she quivered as those rough, warm palms scraped over her bare skin. He zeroed in on the clasp at the front of her bra and released it. Then his hands were on her breasts, and her nipples immediately pebbled in response to his touch. His thumbs circled the rigid peaks, moving slowly and teasingly closer to the aching nubs. She sucked in a breath when his thumbs finally brushed over the hypersensitive tips, and her knees actually trembled.

Because she wasn't entirely sure her legs would continue to support her, she drew him toward the bed and pulled him down onto the mattress with her. His brows winged up, but that was his only response before he captured her mouth again, nibbling on her lower lip as he continued to play with her breasts, driving her ever closer to the edge.

Her fingers were trembling as she worked at the buttons of his shirt, but finally she parted the fabric and touched him. Her hands slid over the ridges of abdominal muscles to his chest, admiring the smooth skin stretched taut over hard muscle. He was a man of so many contrasts. He had the strength to effortlessly control a thousand-pound stallion, the gentleness to bottle-feed an orphaned kitten—and the heart to do so. And when he focused his attention on a woman, he had an uncanny ability to make her feel safe and cherished even as he systematically obliterated any doubts or resistance.

Not that Paige was resisting—or ever had. Because

she'd given her heart to Sutter long before she'd ever offered her body, and he was still in complete command of both. But she knew his body as well as he knew hers, and she stroked her hands over him again, moving down his torso. She unfastened his pants and slid one hand beneath the waistband of his boxers. Here was another contrast: steel encased in velvet. She wrapped her hand around him and was rewarded with a throaty groan.

He pulled back, tugged her sweater over her head and tossed it aside. His shirt followed, then her bra, so that they were both naked from the waist up. She shivered, not from the cold but from the heat in his gaze. And everything inside of her quivered, not with fear but anticipation.

He unfastened her skirt, then shifted back on the mattress so that he could tug it over her hips and down her legs. His eyes followed the progress of the garment, and his lips curved when her silky lace panties and thigh-high stockings were revealed. He traced the lacy edge of the stockings, then his fingertips skimmed over bare flesh to trace the edge of her panties. It was a feather-light caress that arrowed straight to her core.

His eyes lifted to her face, watching her as he traced the same path again. This time his thumb brushed over the thin barrier of lace between her thighs, and she had to bite down on her lip to keep from crying out. He touched her again, and she did gasp now. His lips curved in a slow, satisfied smile. "You're ready already."

She could hardly deny it—and didn't see any reason to. Everything inside her was throbbing, aching, wanting. "It's been a while for me."

"For me, too," he told her.

"More than three years?" she challenged.

"No," he admitted. "But it's been more than five years since I've been with someone who mattered."

And her heart, already precariously perched, toppled over.

"Be with me now," she said, reaching for his pants.

But he caught her hands and gently lowered them back to the bed. "We've waited too long to rush it now."

He tugged her panties down her legs and added them to the growing pile of clothing on the floor. He shifted farther down the mattress, stroking his hands along the outside of her legs, then circling her ankles and sliding her feet back so that her knees were bent and wide. Then he lowered his head between her thighs and zeroed in on her feminine center. It only took one touch—one slow stroke of his tongue—and she shattered.

She cried out, shocked by the immediacy and intensity of the sensations evoked by his touch. The pleasure was so incredible. So overwhelming. It was simply…too much. The release was as much emotional as physical, and as her body was still shuddering with the aftereffects, she felt a tear squeeze from her eye.

But Sutter wasn't nearly finished yet, and he was already driving her toward the next peak. With his lips and his tongue, he nibbled and stroked, deliberately drawing out her pleasure. He'd always known how to take his time, how to extend the enjoyment of lovemaking for both of them. But right now she wanted him so badly that the pleasure was almost painful.

"Sutter…please."

This time she flew. One minute she was lying on her bed, the next she was miles above it, high up in the sky, soaring on the razor's edge of exquisite sensation.

As she floated slowly back toward the ground, his mouth moved up her body. He trailed kisses over her belly, between her breasts. His lips skimmed over a nipple, his tongue swirled around it. And new pleasure started to build all over again.

She reached between their bodies, wrapped her fingers around the hard length of him and stroked him slowly, enticingly. His mouth found hers again, and his tongue slid deep into her mouth then withdrew. A teasing advance and retreat. She arched her back, tilted her hips, wordlessly begging for the completion they both wanted, needed.

"Tell me you want me," he demanded.

"I want you, Sutter. Now."

Always.

But of course she didn't say that aloud. She was going to enjoy what they had together here and now without worrying about tomorrow. There was no past and no future—there was only the present.

He stripped away the last of his clothes and quickly sheathed himself with a condom. Then he rejoined her on the bed, parting her thighs and entering her in one hard thrust. Sex with Sutter had always been good, and she knew that was incredibly rare. He'd been her first love and her first lover, and they'd learned a lot together. While their initial couplings might have been a little hesitant and awkward, they had never been disappointing. Sutter had always been thoughtful and patient, more concerned with her pleasure than his own.

Obviously that hadn't changed. He gave her a moment to catch her breath, then he began to move inside of her. Slow, steady strokes that started the tension building all over again. Long, deep strokes that seemed to touch her very core. Then harder and faster, until their hearts were pounding in tandem and they were racing together toward the ultimate pinnacle of pleasure.

* * *

Somewhere in the midst of the sensual haze that had descended on his brain, Sutter heard something chime. For a moment the sound was completely foreign to him. It sounded again, followed this time by an elbow in his ribs.

"Your phone," Paige mumbled sleepily.

With sincere reluctance, he shifted so that he was sitting up in her bed and reached down to the floor for his pants and the phone that was tucked in one of the pockets.

When he pulled it free, the illuminated screen informed him that he had three new messages. *Three?* He scowled at the phone, but immediately scrolled to his inbox to check the messages.

His annoyance shifted to concern when he realized that they were all from Jenni.

Please call as soon as you get this message.

Need to talk to you ASAP.

Dammit, Sutter, this is important!

He touched his lips to Paige's forehead before he eased away. "I have to make a phone call."

"'Kay," she said, but she didn't move from her face-down position on the bed.

Her hair was spread out over the pillow like an inky spill over pale blue cotton. Her skin was paler—the color of fresh cream, the texture of finest silk. He drew the covers back a little farther than was necessary so that he could admire more of that pale skin, the line of her shoulders, the slope of her spine, the twin dimples low on her back, just above the sweet curve of her buttocks.

She'd always been beautiful, but the skinny girl he'd

first fallen in love with had grown into a very shapely woman. A very passionate woman. And though he sincerely wished the flood had never happened, it was hard to be sorry when it was the event that had brought him home—and back to Paige—again.

"Cold," she murmured.

He tugged the sheet up over her again; she sighed contentedly.

He moved toward the door to have his conversation in the hallway so he wouldn't disturb Paige. He punched the familiar number and the call was answered on the first ring.

"What's going on, Jenni?"

Chapter Fourteen

Jenni?

Though she was admittedly half-asleep and Sutter's voice sounded as if it was coming from far away, Paige had no doubt that she heard him speak another woman's name.

She strained to listen to what he was saying, but he'd closed the door so she could hear the murmur of his voice but wasn't able to decipher any specific words. But she knew that he was on the phone with Jenni—the woman who worked as a trainer at his stables and who drank margaritas. Which proved that their relationship wasn't strictly that of employer and employee.

Not that he'd denied it. In fact, he'd admitted that they were friends, but that description was both vague and open-ended. Especially considering that she'd told her family that she and Sutter were friends—and now she was naked in her bed after tangling up the sheets with him.

She rolled over onto her back and let out an exasperated sigh. She was being ridiculous and she knew it— Sutter wasn't the type of man to take her to bed if he was romantically involved with anyone else. And she'd never been the jealous type. Of course, she'd never had reason to doubt Sutter before. He'd always been the one person she knew she could count on, the one person who would always be there for her. And then he wasn't.

But he was here now, and she wasn't going to spoil what had been a wonderful evening with irrational questions or unfounded accusations. She couldn't deny her curiosity, though, and when he returned to the bedroom, she kept her tone light and asked, "What was that about?"

"I'm not entirely sure," he admitted, snuggling up behind her and wrapping his arms around her. "Jenni was kind of vague on details, aside from the fact that I'd better fix things or start looking for a new trainer."

"What are you going to do?"

"I guess I'm going back to Seattle to fix things—whatever those things are."

"She just calls and you go running?"

"It's my business, Paige. My responsibility."

He didn't even talk to her about it, or ask for her opinion or input. He just made the statement matter-of-factly, as if it should be of no consequence to her. She swallowed. "So when are you going?"

"Tomorrow."

She didn't want to ask, but she had to know if he'd meant what he'd said when he'd promised to stay in Rust Creek Falls. "How long will you be gone?"

"That I don't know," he admitted. "Until I get back and assess the situation, I wouldn't even want to guess."

"Try anyway," she suggested. "Days? Weeks? Months?"

He sighed. "I don't know, but I don't expect it would be too long."

So Paige let it go. Because she couldn't force him to give her an answer, and she couldn't force him to stay. And she was an idiot, because she'd fallen for his smooth lines and sexy smile—hook, line and sinker. And he was leaving her again.

She wanted to bang her head against the wall, but right now her head was cushioned against a nice fluffy pillow and Sutter's arm was wrapped around her middle. She should tell him to go. If he was planning to leave, he might as well go now. Her throat tightened and her eyes burned as she wondered if she was ever going to learn.

Oblivious to her inner turmoil, he snuggled closer and his breathing soon evened out, confirmation that he was sleeping. She stayed in the warm comfort of his arms and tried to convince herself that everything was going to be okay, that this time they would make it. But she couldn't stop the tears that slipped from her eyes.

Sutter woke up alone.

Paige's pillow was still indented from where she'd slept and he could smell her perfume on the sheets, so he figured she hadn't been up for very long. Still, he was disappointed that she'd managed to slip out of bed without waking him. He would have enjoyed easing into the day with her—or easing into her, he thought with a grin.

He sat up in bed, scrubbed his hands over his cheeks. He needed to shower and shave, then he wanted to make love with Paige again. They'd come together several times through the night, and still his body wasn't close to being sated. No matter how many times he had her, it was never enough. He never stopped wanting her.

He considered the possibility that she might be in the shower, but he couldn't hear the water running—which eliminated another one of his fantasies. So he showered alone and shaved with a disposable pink razor he found in the cupboard under the sink, and then he made his way downstairs. "Paige?"

There was no response.

In fact, he suddenly realized there was no sound at all. There was no scent of coffee brewing or breakfast cooking, no footsteps in the kitchen or anywhere else. Then he saw the note propped up on the counter, in front of the empty coffeepot.

It didn't take him long to scan the brief message, and as quickly as he did, his euphoric mood plummeted.

Sutter—
I'm really glad that we've found our way back to being friends again. But as wonderful as last night was, it would be a mistake to let it happen again. What we had was in the past, and I can't let myself think that we have a future together. Have a safe trip back to Seattle and I hope when you come home again that what happened last night doesn't make things awkward between us.
Sincerely,
Paige

Sincerely? For real? He was head over heels in love with her and she'd signed a kiss-off note with an impersonal *sincerely?*

He skimmed the message again as if doing so might enable him to decipher some hidden meaning, because the words on the page didn't make any sense to him.

"...as wonderful as last night was..." Okay, at least she got that part right. Making love with her had been not just wonderful but phenomenal. Even after five years, he'd remembered every little detail of how and where she liked to be touched. And he'd taken great pleasure in pleasuring her, cherishing every soft, sexy sound she made, glorying in the instinctive and sensual movements of her body, loving the way she said his name when he was buried deep inside of her.

"...it would be a mistake to let it happen again." He shook his head over that. It would be a mistake to let it *not* happen again. And he was honestly baffled to think that she could make love with him as openly and passionately as she had the night before and not believe that they were meant to be together.

He refused to accept it. He grabbed his phone and called her cell. After the fourth ring, the call went to her voice mail. He waited five minutes and tried again, but there was still no answer. He tried sending a text message, asking where she was. She ignored it.

He considered tracking her down, and Rust Creek Falls wasn't so big that he couldn't do it. He wanted an explanation—something more than a scribbled note that didn't make any sense to him. If it was really over, he wanted her to look him in the eye and tell him.

He didn't care that he was expected back at Traub Stables. Nothing was more important to him than Paige. But when she failed to answer his third phone call and another text message, he decided that it might be smarter to give her some time. If she was feeling half as churned up inside as he was right now, it might be better for both of them to talk when her emotions had settled.

Since he'd promised to return to Seattle, he would do so, even though he suspected that promise had set Paige off—that she'd assumed his decision to go back to Washington was an indication that he intended to return to his life there. But after last night, how could she not know that his life was with her, wherever she was?

Or maybe her disappearing act this morning had nothing to do with his trip. Maybe she'd simply decided, as she'd stated in her note, that their relationship was in the past and she was ready to move on—without him.

But that explanation didn't sit right with him, either. If she'd made the same claim twenty-four hours earlier, he might have believed it. But the connection between

them when they'd made love had been more than the join-
ing of bodies—it had been the merging of hearts. Yeah,
he knew it sounded corny, but it was true. And that was
why her decision to end things when they were just getting started again completely baffled him.

As much as he puzzled over it, he couldn't come up
with an explanation for Paige's abrupt change of heart.
What he did know was that the next time he saw Paige,
they were going to figure things out once and for all. And
by "figure things out" he meant that he was going to tell
her he loved her, and when she finally admitted that she
loved him, too, he wasn't ever again going to let her go.

But before he could start on the long journey to Seattle, he had one stop to make.

She was a coward.

At the very least, she was weak—especially where
Sutter was concerned. And that was why Paige had
slipped out of her own bed and escaped from her own
house in the early hours of the morning while the man
she loved was still sleeping. Because she couldn't handle
another goodbye. And because she knew that if he took
her in his arms and promised to come back, she would
wait for him, counting the hours, the days, the weeks.
She couldn't—wouldn't—do that again.

There weren't a lot of places that she could go without running into someone she knew, and there were even
fewer places within walking distance. She hadn't considered that his truck was parked behind her car until she
stole out of the house with her keys in hand and realized
she wouldn't be able to get out of the driveway. At that
point, any rational person would reconsider the plan and
perhaps acknowledge that it was both impulsive and des-

perate. But she wasn't feeling very rational; she *was* feeling impulsive and desperate. And so she started to walk.

She didn't have a clear destination in mind, and it was probably by habit more than design that she turned in the direction of the elementary school. But once she thought about it, the school seemed like a logical choice. Because it was a holiday, she knew there wouldn't be many people—if any—at the site today, and she was right.

She made her way down the barren hall to her classroom and looked around at the open space. It wouldn't be too much longer before the desks and cabinets were brought in and displays were tacked up on the pristine walls. But right now it was as empty as Paige felt inside, and she sank down against the wall and let the tears flow.

A long time ago she'd been certain that she'd shed all the tears she was ever going to cry for Sutter Traub— obviously she'd been wrong. She'd had other relationships in the five years that Sutter was gone, but not one of those relationships had ever ended in tears. Because she'd never cared enough about any other man to mourn the end of their relationship.

Apparently she was destined to always love the one man who wouldn't stay with her.

He'd said that he was looking forward to a future with her, but all it took was one phone call from Seattle and he was gone. He hadn't even asked her to go with him this time. Of course, she couldn't have gone if he had asked. She had students who needed her and a lot of preparations still to make before the holidays.

As she wiped at the tears, she accepted that he was already on his way back to Seattle. He'd tried to call, several times in fact, but she hadn't answered any of his calls. In the end he'd sent her a text message, telling her that he was on his way to Seattle and he'd call when he got there. She hadn't responded to that message, either. But she'd taken it as a sign that she could return home without worrying about their paths crossing.

Sure enough, his truck was gone from her driveway when she turned onto North Pine, but she wasn't ready to go into the house yet. Not while the memories of last night were still so fresh in her mind and deeply entrenched in her heart. Groceries, she decided. She needed to stock up on supplies, which meant that she'd have to make a trip into Kalispell.

She'd just turned onto the highway when she realized she was behind a shiny black pickup truck just like Sutter's. Of course, black pickup trucks were hardly an anomaly in Rust Creek Falls, and she chided herself for the instinctive blip in her pulse. But as the vehicle slowed to turn into a driveway, she drew close enough to see the Washington State plate on the bumper.

Washington State plates, on the other hand, *were* anomalies. As she watched his vehicle bump along the long gravel driveway, she felt as if her heart was being squeezed inside her chest.

Apparently Sutter had decided to take a little detour on his way back to Seattle—to Shayla Allen's ranch.

Ten hours later, Sutter finally turned into the drive by the sign that welcomed him to Traub Stables. It was after eight o'clock, so he was surprised to see Jenni's truck still in the lot. Considering that she was invariably at the stables by six every morning, she was working extra late today.

He found her with Midnight Dancer, grooming the horse she'd helped birth two years earlier. She didn't seem particularly worried or stressed about anything, but she didn't seem her usual bubbly self, either.

"So are you going to tell me what's going on?"

"You'll have my letter of resignation tomorrow—consider this my two weeks' notice."

"Why?"

"Because I can't stay here, not if it means I have to work directly with Reese."

"I don't know if my brain's a little slow because I drove five hundred miles today or if this conversation just isn't making any sense to me," he admitted. "There've never been any issues between you before, so why—after three years—do you suddenly have a problem with Reese?"

She met his gaze head-on. "I slept with him."

These were his friends as well as his employees and Sutter liked and respected both of them, but he couldn't deny the protective instinct that rose up in him. "Did he take advantage of you?"

She laughed, though the sound was without humor. "No. Actually I probably took advantage of him."

"Should I be worried about a sexual-harassment suit?"

"I don't think so."

"Okay, you need to give me more information here. Not details," he hastened to clarify. "Please—no details. Just explain to me how you went from sleeping with Reese to wanting to give up a job I know you love."

"Because I love him, too."

"Still not seeing the problem."

She looked away, but not before he saw the shimmer of tears in her eyes. "Reese said it was a mistake—that he never should have let it happen."

Sutter winced.

"See? Even you know that's the wrong thing to say to a woman you were naked with," Jenni noted. "But instead of saying 'wow, that was incredible,' because it was incredible—"

"Details," Sutter reminded her.

"He's more concerned with the fact that our actions would be seen as unprofessional."

"By whom?"

"You."

"You're both adults—what you do on your own time is your business and absolutely none of mine. In fact, I'm quite happy to pretend we never had this conversation."

"I told Reese that's what you would say, but he was adamant. Which means that I'm either in love with a man who values his job more than he values me, or who's looking for an excuse not to get into a relationship. Either way, I can't stay here."

"Please don't make any hasty decisions."

"I'm sorry, Sutter. I know this puts you in a difficult position, but I need to move on."

"Instead of giving me your notice, why don't you take a vacation?" he suggested.

Her brows lifted. "That's your solution?"

"You've been working hard for the past few years—and even harder over the past several months. You deserve some time off, a break from the routines."

"A break from Reese, you mean?"

He shrugged. "Maybe what he needs is some time to think about what his life would be like without you in it."

"And maybe he'll decide he likes it better that way."

"If he does, then he doesn't deserve you."

She sighed. "Do you really think it will work?"

"I don't know," he admitted. "I'm probably the last person who should be giving relationship advice."

"Why do you say that?"

"Because it seems that I keep screwing up with the

only woman I've ever loved—and I actually thought things were back on track."

"This would be the girl you left behind when you first moved out to Seattle?" Jenni asked.

Sutter nodded. "But only after I asked her to come with me, and she said no."

"And when you started to get things back on track—and by that, I assume you mean you got her back into bed," she said drily, "you left her again."

"Because you called and said I was needed here."

Now it was her turn to wince. "You slept with her and then left because of a call from another woman?"

"It wasn't like that," he protested.

"It sounds exactly like that to me," she told him. "And I'm sure that's how it sounded to her."

Sutter scowled. "Then she wasn't listening to what I was saying, because I told her I would be back."

"Did you tell her when?"

"I could hardly give her a firm return date when I didn't know how long it would take to work things out here."

"You also didn't say, 'I'll be gone for a few days—a week at most—but I'm coming back to you.'"

"You think that would have made a difference?"

She huffed out an exasperated breath. "You're as much an idiot as Reese."

"At least I know what I want," he said. "Which is why I'm thinking about making a permanent move back to Rust Creek Falls." His thoughts shifted to his meeting with Shayla Allen—had it really only been earlier that morning? So much had happened since he'd awakened alone in Paige's bed that he felt as if days had passed.

He frowned now, realizing that although it hadn't been days, a lot of hours had passed and he still hadn't heard from Paige. She hadn't returned any of his calls or responded to any of his text messages, which wasn't really surprising. Based on the letter she'd left for him, she was trying to cut all ties between them. He had no intention of letting that happen.

"What would you do in Rust Creek Falls?"

He gestured to encompass the stables. "Something like this."

"Then you'll need a trainer there," she noted hopefully.

"Probably. But I *know* I need a trainer here."

She shook her head. "I'm going to check online for an all-inclusive in Maui."

Though it wasn't what he wanted to hear, he figured it was a compromise he had to accept—at least for now. He couldn't imagine Traub Stables without her, but if she insisted on leaving... "Would you really be willing to move to Montana?"

"I'd prefer Florida," she said. "But Montana would suffice."

"Why Florida?"

"Because it's as far away from Seattle as you can get while still staying in the country."

"Okay, then. I'll figure out what's going on in Montana and let you know."

"She must be one special lady," Jenni noted.

Sutter had no doubt that she was, even when she was driving him completely crazy. "I've never known anyone like her," he admitted.

"So who's going to handle things around here if I suddenly decide to take a trip to Maui?"

"I will."

"I thought you were anxious to get back to Montana?"

"I was," he agreed. "But I've decided that someone else needs some time to think."

* * *

Paige's cards had been sent, her cookies were baked and her house was decorated—aside from the tree, which she would get two weeks before Christmas. Though she spent the day with her family, she still liked to put up her own tree. Christmas was her absolute favorite time of the year—she loved everything about the holiday, especially the fact that she had all kinds of things to keep her busy and absolutely no time to waste thinking about Sutter Traub. But that didn't stop her from thinking about him anyway.

She went shopping in Kalispell with Lindsay. She'd invited both of her sisters to make the trip with her, but Lani had already committed to babysitting for a friend who needed to shop without her kids in tow.

"When's Sutter coming back?" Lindsay waited until they were resting their feet after a marathon trek through the toy store and savoring gingerbread lattes before she asked the question that Paige had been anticipating all day.

"I don't know that he is."

Her sister frowned. "Haven't you talked to him?"

"Not since the day after Thanksgiving." More specifically, not since the morning after they'd made love, but she wasn't going to share that information with Lindsay.

"He hasn't called?"

"He's called," she admitted. "Every day."

"You're not taking his calls," Lindsay guessed.

"I don't know what to say to him."

"How about 'I love you. Please come home'?"

"Except that Seattle is his home now," she reminded her sister—and herself.

"You wouldn't know it from the amount of time he's spent in Rust Creek Falls over the past four months."

"Yeah, it fooled me, too," Paige admitted.

"You fell in love with him again, didn't you?" Lindsay said, her tone just a little wistful.

She sighed. "I don't think I ever stopped."

"And yet you're still here when he's in Washington?"

"I have a job here, responsibilities I can't just abandon."

"Then why are you mad at Sutter for not abandoning his?"

"I'm not mad at Sutter."

"You're not taking his calls," Lindsay reminded her.

"I'm…confused," she admitted.

"Probably not half as confused as he is."

"Why would he be confused?"

"Because less than a week ago he was in your bed and now you're giving him the silent treatment."

Paige's jaw dropped. "He wasn't— I'm not—" She blew out a breath. "How did you know?"

"Are you kidding? When you left with him on Thanksgiving, the heat between the two of you was practically melting your clothes away before you were out the door."

"Okay, yes, he spent the night with me."

"So what really happened to cause this one-eighty?"

"He got a phone call from his trainer and practically leaped out of bed to race back to her." If it had been a genuine crisis at the stable—a sick horse, a disgruntled client, an employee embezzling funds—she would have understood the urgency of the situation. Instead, it was his trainer. His beautiful, blond, female trainer.

Not that he'd described Jenni to her in that way. In fact, he hadn't given her any details about the woman he claimed was a friend as well as a valued employee. So Paige had looked her up and discovered that Traub Stables had its own website, including bios and photos

of the employees—and that Jenni Locke was undeniably gorgeous.

Paige had never had any reason not to trust Sutter.
In high school there had been a lot of girls who'd liked
him. All of the Traub brothers had been popular and had
drawn attention wherever they went. But while she and
Sutter were together, Paige had never doubted his commitment to her.

Everything was different now, though. The fact that
they'd slept together didn't mean there was a commitment between them, especially when he'd left the state
the very next morning.

"I'd be upset, too, if that's what really happened,"
Lindsay said. "But I've seen the way Sutter looks at
you—the man's as head over heels as you are—and if he
raced back to Seattle, it was because his *trainer* needed
him to be there and not because a woman crooked her
finger.

"But if that's what you really believe," she continued,
"why not just cut your losses and move on? Why are you
so miserable without him?"

"I know I should move on. My head is telling me to
forget about him, that this emergency that called him
back to Seattle was a timely reminder of the fact that we
have separate lives, in separate cities. But my heart—"
She sighed again. "My heart refuses to let go."

"Then maybe it's time you started listening to your
heart," her sister said gently. "Go to Seattle, tell Sutter
how you feel and figure out a way to make this work."

Paige wished it was that easy. But when he'd decided
to go back to Seattle without even talking to her, she'd
realized that she wasn't as important to him as his business. Even if he did love her, he didn't love her enough
to put her first, so she shook her head.

Lindsay shook her head. "You were happy with him, and you're obviously miserable without him. If I was in your situation, you can bet I'd do whatever was necessary to be with the man I loved."

"There's one other thing I didn't tell you," Paige admitted now.

"What's that?"

"He didn't race straight back to Seattle. He made a detour first."

"What kind of detour?" her sister asked curiously.

"To Shayla Allen's ranch."

"Well, that *is* interesting."

"Interesting?" Paige said skeptically.

Shayla Allen was a young widow who didn't know the first thing about ranching, and most people in Rust Creek Falls had assumed she would sell off the property her husband had left to her when he died. So far she'd avoided doing so, and there seemed to be a regular parade of handsome cowboys stopping by the ranch to help her with one thing or another.

"Really, Paige, green is not your color," Lindsay chided.

"Because there's got to be a reasonable explanation for Sutter's visit to her ranch?" she challenged.

"There could be," her sister said. "It's not common knowledge yet, but Shayla has decided to sell the ranch and move back East. So it's possible that Sutter wasn't there to check out her assets but her real estate."

Chapter Fifteen

After she dropped Lindsay off with her assortment of packages, Paige's stomach was rumbling. Because she didn't feel like cooking, she decided to stop by the Ace in the Hole to grab a quick bite. She didn't usually venture into the bar on her own, but she hadn't been in the mood for any more company tonight—especially not the company of either of her sisters. Since Sutter had left town, Lani's smug "I told you so" attitude had been more than a little obnoxious. Lindsay was more empathetic, but her quiet understanding and sincere sympathy made Paige want to cry—and she'd done enough of that already.

She walked into the Ace in the Hole and realized there wasn't an unoccupied table in the whole place. There were a couple of empty stools at the bar, but she wouldn't feel comfortable sitting there with a bunch of men she didn't know.

And then she saw Alex.

He, too, seemed to be alone, but he'd managed to find a table. She took two steps in his direction before she changed her mind. She didn't want to put him in the awkward position of having to offer her a seat if he preferred solitude. Except that he looked up then and caught her eye, and immediately beckoned her over. The complete lack of hesitation in his response assured her that there wouldn't be any awkwardness between them, and she made her way over.

"Busy place tonight," Paige commented.

He nodded. "I managed to snag this table as a group of people was leaving. There's plenty of room if you want to join me."

"Thanks." She slid into the seat across from him. "Have you ordered already?"

He shook his head. "I was thinking about the nachos grande, but the platter's too big for one person."

"Nachos grande sounds good to me."

Alex ordered a beer; Paige stuck with soda. They chatted as they ate—about business at the mill, the progress at the school and various other local issues. It was casual and easy and Paige wondered how she'd ever thought they might have a future together when her feelings for him had always been so equable.

It wasn't until they were almost finished with the nachos that Paige noticed Dallas Traub was at the bar, deep in discussion with another man she recognized from the Triple T. A few minutes later he stood up, shook the man's hand, then turned and looked directly at her.

Paige lifted her hand to wave; his only response was a scathing glance before he headed to the door.

"Excuse me for a minute," Paige said to Alex, grabbing her jacket and hurrying after Sutter's brother.

She pushed open the screen door and stepped out. "Dallas, wait!"

He halted, then reluctantly turned back to face her. "If you want me to lie to my brother about what I saw tonight—forget it."

She was taken aback by the vehemence of his tone as much as the implication of his words, but she hadn't chased after him to have an argument in the parking lot. "While I have to admit to some curiosity about what you think you saw, I just wanted to give you something that I picked up in Kalispell today."

She shoved her arms into the sleeves of her coat as she started toward her car, and though Dallas still looked skeptical, he followed. Paige rifled through the assortment of bags in her trunk until she found the biggest one—from the toy store. She pulled out the box she wanted and handed it to Dallas.

"What is this?"

She huffed out a breath. "Did you even look at the letter Robbie wrote to Santa?"

"Of course," he said automatically.

And maybe he had looked at it, but he obviously hadn't made note of his son's request.

"Then you should know that this is a deluxe neon alien-invasion spaceship, which happens to be one of the hottest new toys this year. The girl who was unpacking the box in the store said they haven't been able to keep them in stock."

And because of that, she'd bought two—one for Robbie and one for the unnamed eight-year-old boy whose tag she had taken off of the Tree of Hope at Crawford's.

"I'm sorry if I overstepped," she said, perhaps a little stiffly. "But I didn't want to take a chance that you might not be able to find one, and it was really the only thing Robbie wanted. Well, aside from a new mommy."

He kept his gaze focused on the toy, and when he spoke again, his voice had lost most of the edge it usually carried when he was talking to her. "In that case, I guess I should say thank you. And ask how much—"

"It's a gift," she said, cutting off his question. "For Robbie from Santa."

He nodded. "Then thank you again."

"You're welcome." She closed the trunk of her car again and turned to go back into the bar.

Sutter hadn't planned to be in Seattle for more than a couple of days. His conversation with Jenni convinced him to stay longer, not just because he'd promised to cover for her so that she could take a vacation but because he needed some time to figure out his plans for his future. A future he wanted to spend with Paige.

Except that she continued to dodge his calls and ignore his text messages. He figured the advice he'd given to Jenni about Reese could apply to his relationship with Paige, as well. So he was giving her some time to think about everything that had happened between them and figure out where he fit into her life and her future. Because the contents of her letter notwithstanding, he didn't believe for a minute that her feelings for him were in the past.

But he missed her. With every day that passed, he missed her more. He tried to focus on business, catching up on everything that had happened while he was away, communicating with clients and making sure that Jenni's assistants were handling their numerous duties and responsibilities. He was pleased to note that they seemed to adjust to her absence just fine. Reese, on the other hand, was as grumpy as a bear rudely awakened from deep hibernation.

Sutter reminded himself that it was none of his business. Either they would figure things out for themselves or they wouldn't—it had nothing to do with him. Nothing aside from the fact that he could lose the best trainer he'd ever known.

Or he could take her to Montana with him. Because the more he thought about it, the more convinced he was that he could do what he was doing in Seattle back home in Rust Creek Falls. On Wednesday he got a fax from Shayla Allen's real estate agent with her acceptance of his offer on the property. He'd been expecting a counteroffer, some haggling back and forth that would draw out the process for a week or more. He hadn't expected it would be that easy, but apparently the owner was serious about selling and moving on, and now Sutter had a ranch—and a hefty mortgage—in Rust Creek Falls and no firm plans for either it or his business in Seattle.

He wanted to talk to Paige, to discuss his plans with her. It occurred to him, albeit belatedly, that they should have had a conversation *before* he put the offer in on the Allen ranch. Because Paige had been the primary factor in his decision to move back to Rust Creek Falls, and he hoped she would be pleased to learn about his plan.

But first she had to get over being mad at him—and according to Jenni, she had reason to be. Apparently he should have reassured her that he would be back, told her he would miss her unbearably and promised to love her forever.

Maybe he was an idiot—and according to Jenni, he was—but he'd thought all of that was implied. With every touch of his hands and his lips and his body when they'd made love, he'd told her that he loved her. And though neither of them had spoken the words, he'd been certain she was saying the same thing back.

But—according to Jenni again—he'd negated all of that by leaving town, hence her completely justified determination to push him out of her life forever. But this time, Sutter wasn't going to be pushed anywhere.

And he wasn't going to let her continue to ignore him, either. He decided that flowers would get her attention again, but in honor of the holiday season he ordered poinsettias this time—one for each Christmas that they'd spent apart. And he arranged for them to be delivered one at a time.

She might not be pleased by the interruptions to her schedule, but at least he'd have her attention.

The first delivery didn't come with a card. Neither did the second or the third. When the doorbell interrupted her teaching for a fourth time Friday afternoon, Paige demanded that the deliveryman tell her who had sent the flowers. He just shrugged and said, "I don't take the orders. I just deliver them."

When the bell rang again at two o'clock and she found the same deliveryman with yet another poinsettia, she was ready to scream. But he spoke before she could say— or scream—anything.

"There's a card with this one," he told her.

She forced a smile. "In that case, thank you."

As her class was finishing up a geography test, she took a moment to pry the card from the envelope. "One poinsettia for every Christmas that we were apart—and the last one I'll ever send."

It wasn't signed, but she knew it was from Sutter. She'd suspected, of course, even after the first one, because she couldn't remember the last time anyone else had sent her flowers. The cryptic reference to the five years they were apart confirmed it.

But what, exactly, did the message mean? Was he saying that they wouldn't ever have to spend another Christmas apart? And did that mean he was coming back to Rust Creek Falls?

Hope flared in her heart like a match first struck, but it burned out just as quickly. Because even if he was coming home again— For how long this time? How long would he stay before something else called him away again? She didn't want to live her life in a state of uncertainty.

But she didn't want to live her life without him, either. Because there was one thing she knew for sure: she was still, and always would be, in love with Sutter Traub.

And after dinner with her parents tonight, she was going to tell them about her decision to book a flight to Washington.

Sutter left Seattle before Jenni got back from Maui, because when Reese had asked for her flight information so that he could pick her up from the airport, he'd figured his stable manager had everything under control. And now it was time for him to take control of his life and his future. As he drove back to Montana, he tried to plan out his every action and word—he didn't anticipate arriving back in Rust Creek Falls to find Paige's driveway empty and her house in darkness.

It was just around dinnertime on a Friday night, which led him to the obvious conclusion that she'd gone somewhere to eat. Probably not the Ace in the Hole, since Dallas had told him that she'd been there earlier in the week with Alex Monroe. His brother's tone had implied that it was a date, but Sutter didn't believe it. Paige wasn't the type of woman to string someone along, so he knew she wouldn't be on a date with the other man only a few weeks after ending their relationship—and so soon after taking Sutter to her bed.

He figured her parents' house was the most likely place to find her—and the absolute last place he wanted to go considering his reception there on Thanksgiving. But he would follow Paige to the ends of the earth if he had to. Of course, the ends of the earth—wherever that might be—was, in many ways, preferable to the Dalton home, but he turned his truck in that direction anyway.

He wasn't looking for another confrontation, but as he knocked on the door, he braced himself for the possibility.

"What are you doing here?" Ben Dalton asked.

Sutter refused to be dissuaded by either the chilly tone or dismissive glance. He held the older man's gaze and said, "I need to see Paige."

"Why?"

"I have some things I need to say to her."

"I can pass on a message."

"Oh, for goodness' sake, Dad. Let him come in."

Sutter sent a quick, grateful smile to Lindsay. Ben scowled but stepped away from the door. Lani stood on the other side of her father, her arms folded across her chest. Mary stood behind her daughter, a worried frown on her face.

Great—it seemed that he had an audience, including every female member of the Dalton family except the one he most wanted to see.

"Since you're all here—I have something to say to you, too," Sutter told them. "I made some mistakes in the past, and it took me a while to acknowledge those mistakes and move on, but I hope you can do the same, because I'm not the same guy I was when I left town five years ago."

"Haven't seen much evidence of anything different," Ben said.

"You will," he promised Paige's father. "But there is one thing that hasn't changed in all of the years that I was gone—and that's how I feel about your daughter."

"How *do* you feel about her?" Lani demanded.

"Jeez, Lani, could you butt out of my life for five minutes?" Paige demanded, stepping into the room.

She was wearing one of those long skirts she seemed to favor, this one in a swirling pattern of cream and chocolate, with a cream-colored tunic-style sweater. Her cheeks were a little paler than usual and there were dark smudges beneath her eyes, and he wondered if they might be proof that she'd suffered as many sleepless nights as he had. But she was still the most beautiful woman he'd ever known, and looking at her now, his heart actually ached with wanting.

He shifted his gaze to her sister. "I don't have a problem answering your question," he told Lani. "Because I love Paige."

She looked unconvinced, but Lindsay sighed and pressed a hand to her heart. Mary worried her lip and Ben's scowl deepened.

But Sutter didn't care about any of their responses. He turned to Paige again. "It's true," he told her. "I love you."

Her eyes filled with tears, but she said nothing and made no move toward him.

So he stepped forward and took her hand. Her fingers were ice-cold and trembling. He squeezed gently. "I love you, Paige, with my whole heart. I always have and I always will."

A single tear trembled on the edge of her lashes, then tracked slowly down her cheek. His heart turned over in his chest. Whatever reaction he'd expected, it wasn't that his declaration would make her cry.

"I mean it, Paige." He was speaking only to her now, oblivious to the fact that her parents and sisters were still in the room. He dropped to one knee beside her. "I've never stopped loving you, and I never want to leave you again. I want to build a life with you, here in Rust Creek Falls. I'm hoping that's what you want, too, and that this time you'll say yes, because I'm asking you to marry me."

* * *

Paige hadn't expected to see Sutter tonight. And she certainly hadn't expected such a heartfelt declaration—or a proposal. Yes, she loved him, and yes, she'd been willing to go to Seattle to meet him on his turf to talk about the possibility of a future for them together—because that was what she wanted more than anything. But now that he was here, offering her everything she'd always wanted, she was almost too afraid to reach out and take it.

"Okay, I can understand why you'd have some reservations," Sutter said when she failed to respond. "Because I was still carrying a lot of baggage from what happened five years ago—not just with you, but with my family. And I know I wasted a lot of years feeling hurt and angry and guilty, but I'm not going to waste any more. I know I can't do anything to give us back those five years, but I'm ready to move forward now, and I really want to do that with you by my side."

It was the sincerity in his gaze as much as the earnestness in his voice that finally propelled her to action. She lifted a trembling hand to his lips, halting the flow of words so that she could speak.

"Yes," she said softly.

His lips curved, just a little. "Yes?"

She nodded. "I love you, Sutter, I always have. And I want to move forward with you, too."

"Does that mean I can get off my knee?"

"Don't I get the ring first?"

He dipped a hand into his pocket. "How did you know I had a ring?"

"You got down on one knee."

He was smiling as he retrieved the ring and slid it onto the third finger of her left hand. The exquisite emerald-cut diamond at the center was flanked by slightly smaller but equally stunning tapered baguettes. "I wanted something with three stones," he said. "To represent our past, our present and our future."

"It's perfect," she said. "But all I want—all I *need*—is you."

Finally he rose to his feet and kissed her. And in that touch of his mouth against hers, all the questions and doubts and loneliness of the past week faded away.

It was only when she heard both Lani and Lindsay sigh that she remembered they weren't alone. Reluctantly, she eased her lips from his and turned to face her parents.

"It looks like we're going to need that extra leaf in the table for Christmas," Mary said to her husband.

Ben nodded. "And for every holiday thereafter."

Their comments weren't exactly an overwhelming endorsement of Paige and Sutter's engagement, but they did represent a significant shift in her parents' attitudes from Thanksgiving, and that was a good start. Then her father took a step forward.

"You make my daughter happy and those mistakes of the past will be forgotten," he said.

And when he offered Sutter his hand, Paige saw her mother's eyes fill with tears.

"I will," Sutter said, and shook to seal his promise.

"Isn't that what you're supposed to say at the wedding?" Lindsay teased.

Sutter grinned at her. "I'm practicing."

"About the wedding," Mary began.

"*Later,* Mom," Paige said firmly. "Let me get used to being engaged first."

"All right," her mother relented. "But planning a wedding takes time—there are so many details to take care of."

But the only detail Paige was thinking about right

now was how to discreetly make a quick exit so that she and Sutter could celebrate their engagement in private.

Her fiancé, obviously on the same wavelength, said, "Before we start talking about wedding dates, I think my parents would like to know about this turn of events."

"Oh, right. Of course," Mary agreed.

So they said goodbye to her family and headed out to share the good news with his. But on the way, they decided to stop at Paige's house.

They did eventually get around to telling Sutter's family about their engagement—but not until much later the following morning.

Epilogue

Three weeks later, with the now-familiar weight of her engagement ring on her finger, Paige escaped with Sutter to Seattle for the weekend. Since the publicity from Lissa's writing had sent a mass of volunteers to Rust Creek Falls to help with the town's restoration and the new school was almost complete, they were finally able to take some time for themselves without feeling guilty.

Paige was excited to see Seattle, but mostly she was eager to get a glimpse of the life Sutter had built for himself in the city. Traub Stables was quite an impressive facility, including a thirty-stall barn, a breeding shed, an indoor riding arena, neatly fenced paddocks and even a spa to help rehabilitate injured horses. And all of the buildings were decked out for the holiday season with miles of pine garlands, enormous evergreen wreaths and countless twinkling white lights.

Not only were the buildings and grounds well maintained, but the horses she saw were all in prime condition, a testament to the quality of care they received. On the tour she also got to meet Jenni and Reese, and found out that they weren't just friends of Sutter's and employees at the stables but also recently engaged.

"You've done an incredible job here," she told Sutter.

"I didn't have to do a lot," he said. "The buildings

were in pretty good shape when I bought the property, so they needed more hands-on attention than major construction. And I got lucky that I made so many contacts when I was working at Rolling Meadows."

"You're being modest," she chided. "This place is really impressive."

"I'm proud of it," he admitted.

"It makes me wonder how you could want to leave here—to give up something that you obviously poured so much of your heart and soul into."

He put his arms around her. "Don't you know that my heart and soul are yours? Spending my life with you means that I'm not giving anything up—I'm getting everything I ever wanted."

"But if I hadn't been so insistent on staying in Rust Creek Falls, would you have chosen to live here?"

"I want to be with you, Paige."

"Reese seems like he's more than qualified to handle the day-to-day operations of the business."

"And has been since the summer," Sutter agreed. "If he wanted it, I'd sell the place to him."

"He doesn't want it?"

"He claims he's not ready for the responsibility of ownership—or the risks. He's happy to do what he does and isn't ready to take on the kind of mortgage he would need to take it off my hands."

"What if you were partners?" she suggested. "You could maintain an interest in the business but he'd continue to be responsible for the day-to-day operations."

It was an interesting suggestion and, in some ways, an obvious solution. But he was curious. "Why are you suddenly reluctant for me to sell?"

She shrugged. "I just thought it might be nice to have a place where we could get away, and it would give our children the opportunity to experience both country life and city living."

Something in her deliberately casual tone triggered his radar, making him suspect that her comment wasn't as offhand as she wanted him to think. "Children?"

"We used to talk about having kids," she reminded him. "Is that still what you want?"

"Yeah, that's still what I want." He tipped her chin up. "Are you...pregnant?"

"I don't know, but I think...I might be."

Sutter whooped with joy and wrapped his arms around her.

She laughed as he spun her around. "And to think I had some concerns about how you'd react to the news."

He set her back on her feet and tipped her chin up to brush his lips over hers. "Now can we set a date for the wedding?"

She chuckled. "I guess we'd better."

"When?"

"March," she suggested. "Then we can go on our honeymoon during spring break."

"How about we have the wedding in January and the honeymoon in March?"

"Afraid if we wait too long I might change my mind?"

He shook his head. "Nope. I don't have any doubts about anything anymore. I just want to start our life together as soon as possible."

She lifted her arms to link them behind his head, drawing his mouth down to hers. "Then I guess we're getting married in January."

As Sutter kissed his bride to be under the mistletoe, he couldn't help but marvel at all the things he had to be thankful for—because of the woman in his arms.

* * * * *

Don't miss THE MAVERICK'S CHRISTMAS BABY by USA TODAY *bestselling author Victoria Pade, the next installment in the new Special Edition continuity* MONTANA MAVERICKS: RUST CREEK COWBOYS *On sale December 2013, wherever Harlequin books are sold.*

REQUEST YOUR FREE BOOKS!
2 FREE NOVELS PLUS 2 FREE GIFTS!

⊕ HARLEQUIN®

SPECIAL EDITION

Life, Love & Family

YES! Please send me 2 FREE Harlequin® Special Edition novels and my 2 FREE gifts (gifts are worth about $10). After receiving them, if I don't wish to receive any more books, I can return the shipping statement marked "cancel." If I don't cancel, I will receive 6 brand-new novels every month and be billed just $4.74 per book in the U.S. or $5.24 per book in Canada. That's a savings of at least 14% off the cover price! It's quite a bargain! Shipping and handling is just 50¢ per book in the U.S. and 75¢ per book in Canada.* I understand that accepting the 2 free books and gifts places me under no obligation to buy anything. I can always return a shipment and cancel at any time. Even if I never buy another book, the two free books and gifts are mine to keep forever.

235/335 HDN F45Y

Name	(PLEASE PRINT)

Address	Apt. #

City	State/Prov.	Zip/Postal Code

Signature (if under 18, a parent or guardian must sign)

Mail to the **Harlequin® Reader Service:**
IN U.S.A.: P.O. Box 1867, Buffalo, NY 14240-1867
IN CANADA: P.O. Box 609, Fort Erie, Ontario L2A 5X3

Want to try two free books from another line?
Call 1-800-873-8635 or visit www.ReaderService.com.

* Terms and prices subject to change without notice. Prices do not include applicable taxes. Sales tax applicable in N.Y. Canadian residents will be charged applicable taxes. Offer not valid in Quebec. This offer is limited to one order per household. Not valid for current subscribers to Harlequin Special Edition books. All orders subject to credit approval. Credit or debit balances in a customer's account(s) may be offset by any other outstanding balance owed by or to the customer. Please allow 4 to 6 weeks for delivery. Offer available while quantities last.

Your Privacy—The Harlequin® Reader Service is committed to protecting your privacy. Our Privacy Policy is available online at www.ReaderService.com or upon request from the Harlequin Reader Service.

We make a portion of our mailing list available to reputable third parties that offer products we believe may interest you. If you prefer that we not exchange your name with third parties, or if you wish to clarify or modify your communication preferences, please visit us at www.ReaderService.com/consumerschoice or write to us at Harlequin Reader Service Preference Service, P.O. Box 9062, Buffalo, NY 14269. Include your complete name and address.

HSEI3R

Damien Bravo-Calabretti was the
Playboy Prince of Montedoro, until innocent Lucy Cordell
asked Dami to be her first. Will this bad-boy prince fall for
the sweet beauty under the mistletoe?

***

She shook that finger at him again. "Dami, I may be inexperienced, but I saw the look on your face. I felt your arms around me. I felt…everything. I know that you liked kissing me. You liked it and that made you realize that you *could* make love with me, after all. That you could do it and even enjoy it. And that wasn't what you meant to do, when you told me we could have the weekend together. That ruined your plan—the plan I have been totally up on right from the first—your plan to show me a nice time and send me back to America as ignorant of lovemaking as I was when I got here."

"Luce…"

"Just answer the question, please."

"I have absolutely no idea what the question was."

"Did you like kissing me?"

Now he was the one gulping like some green boy. "Didn't *you* already answer that for me?"

"I did, yeah. But I would also like to have you answer it for yourself."

He wanted to get up and walk out of the room. But more than that, he wanted what she kept insisting *she* wanted. He wanted to take off her floppy sweater, her skinny jeans and her pink tennis shoes. He wanted to see her naked body. And take her in his arms. And carry her to his bed and show her all the pleasures she was so hungry to discover.

"Dami. Did you like kissing me?"

"Damn you," he said, low.

And then she said nothing. That shocked the hell out of him. Lucy. Not saying a word. Not waving her hands around. Simply sitting there with her big sweater drooping off one silky shoulder, daring him with her eyes to open his mouth and tell her the truth.

He never could resist a dare. "Yes, Luce. I did. I liked kissing you. I liked it very much."

***

We hope you enjoyed this sneak peek from
USA TODAY *bestselling author Christine Rimmer's new Harlequin Special Edition book,* **HOLIDAY ROYALE,** *the next installment in her popular miniseries The Bravo Royales, on sale December 2013, wherever Harlequin books are sold!*

⬧ **HARLEQUIN**®

SPECIAL EDITION

Life, Love and Family

It's a white Christmas in Rust Creek Falls—and
USA TODAY bestselling author Victoria Pade
weaves the perfect holiday romance between
a single dad and the soon-to-be-mom
he just can't resist, in
THE MAVERICK'S CHRISTMAS BABY

Single and pregnant, Nina Crawford finds herself
in trouble when she meets her family's archrival,
handsome Dallas Traub. Can Mr. Cowboy and
Ms. Crawford survive feuding families, three
boisterous boys and a little bundle of joy intent on
an early arrival? Snuggle up, Maverick fans, for the
heartwarming conclusion of Rust Creek Cowboys!

*Available in December from
Harlequin® Special Edition®, wherever books are sold.*

HSE65783

A COLD CREEK
CHRISTMAS SURPRISE

When Haven Whitmore is injured on
Ridge Bowman's ranch, Ridge steps up—and falls
for her. Whether this tantalizing twosome can make
it work will depend on whether they can put to rest
the Ghosts of Relationships Past.

*Look for the conclusion of
The Cowboys of Cold Creek miniseries
from RaeAnne Thayne next month,
from Harlequin® Special Edition®!*

Available wherever books and ebooks are sold.

Love the Harlequin book you just read?

Your opinion matters.

Review this book on your favorite book site, review site, blog or your own social media properties and share your opinion with other readers!

Be sure to connect with us at:
Harlequin.com/Newsletters
Facebook.com/HarlequinBooks
Twitter.com/HarlequinBooks